He had fantasized about what they could have had....

A lopsided snowman in the front yard. No, this would have never been his home. Ever since his parents had been murdered in their beds on Christmas Eve, Thad had never had a home, or at least he'd never let any place feel like one.

But Thad needed an angel now. As much as he needed to leave Caroline alone, he needed even more to see her face.

She wasn't the one who opened the door at his knock, though.

At first it looked as though it had swung open of its own volition, until Thad adjusted his line of vision way down to the little boy who stood in the doorway. With his dark brown hair and blue eyes, the kid was a miniature version of Thad.

Caroline had had his son.

LISA CHILDS

DADDY BOMBSHELL

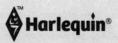

Harlequin®

TORONTO NEW YORK LONDON
AMSTERDAM PARIS SYDNEY HAMBURG
STOCKHOLM ATHENS TOKYO MILAN MADRID
PRAGUE WARSAW BUDAPEST AUCKLAND

To Melissa Jeglinski for being a wonderful, supportive friend as well as an amazing agent!

Special thanks and acknowledgment to Lisa Childs for her contribution to the Situation: Christmas series.

Recycling programs for this product may not exist in your area.

ISBN-13: 978-0-373-74639-2

DADDY BOMBSHELL

Copyright © 2011 by Harlequin Books S.A.

ABOUT THE AUTHOR

Bestselling, award-winning author Lisa Childs writes paranormal and contemporary romance for Harlequin Books. She lives on thirty acres in west Michigan with her husband, two daughters, a talkative Siamese and a long-haired Chihuahua who thinks she's a Rottweiler. Lisa loves hearing from readers, who can contact her through her website, www.lisachilds.com, or snail mail address, P.O. Box 139, Marne, MI 49435.

Books by Lisa Childs

HARLEQUIN INTRIGUE

CAST OF CHARACTERS

Thad Kendall—The youngest son of St. Louis's infamously murdered couple, he's more than the photojournalist everyone thinks he is, and in the course of his real job, he's made enemies. One of those enemies may be threatening Thad now…or maybe it's his parents' real killer, whom he's determined to finally bring to justice.

Caroline Emerson—Four years ago, the elementary school teacher fell for one of the elite Kendalls of St. Louis, even though she knew he was keeping secrets and that he would leave her—that's why she's determined not to fall for him again. But she's been keeping a secret of her own that binds them together forever.

Mark Emerson—The three-year-old boy wants only one thing for Christmas: a real family.

Wade—The man with no known last name was stalking Thad's sister until Thad killed him. Now someone's stalking Thad and those who mean the most to him.

Len Michaels—The tortured spy may have given up Thad's real identity before his death, putting Thad and everyone he cares about in imminent danger.

Anya Smith—Thad's handler at the State Department will eliminate any potential liability to her operation.

The Christmas Eve killer—Two decades ago he murdered in an impulsive fit of rage, now he's older, more controlled and infinitely more dangerous—and determined to kill again on Christmas Eve.

Chapter One

His finger twitched and, as if by reflex alone, he squeezed the trigger. The gun vibrated in his hand as the bullet propelled down the barrel. He didn't miss.

He never did....

The body dropped facedown onto the flagstones of the patio. Blood saturated clothing and pooled on the patio beneath the body.

Thad Kendall closed the distance between them and hunched down, feeling for a pulse. Nothing flickered beneath the skin, which was already growing cold despite the heat of the fire that was burning down the cottage on the other side of the patio.

Who the hell was this person who had set fire to the cottage and killed the man near the front of the cottage—not to mention fired all those shots that Thad had barely dodged?

He drew in a deep breath of acrid smoke.

Then he reached out and rolled the body over so he could see the face. His sister's distinctive green eyes, wide with shock, stared up at him.

"No!" Thad awoke with the shout and jerked upright in bed. He had already kicked off the covers, and a fine sheen of sweat covered his chest and back. The perspiration chilled him nearly as much as the dream had.

But it wasn't just a dream; it was a memory of the shooting that had happened a week ago.

A knock rapped softly against his door, but before he could clear his throat to respond, it creaked open. "You okay?" a feminine voice gently asked.

He grabbed up a T-shirt from beside the bed and dragged it over his head. "Yeah, yeah…"

Just as she hadn't hesitated before opening the door, she didn't hesitate before crossing the room and sitting on his bed. "You were yelling," she said. "Did you have a bad dream?"

Thad stared into his sister's wide green eyes, which were full of concern and—thank God—life. He hadn't shot her that night, and the man he had shot hadn't really had her eyes. His had been a flat brown color, but something about the size and shape of them—as well as the man's other features—had reminded Thad so much of Natalie that the image had haunted him ever since he'd turned the body over.

"The worst…"

She shuddered. "I know what that's like."

He snaked an arm around her shoulders. "Yes, you do."

Twenty years ago, Natalie had found their parents dead in their beds on Christmas morning, and even though she later hadn't remembered finding their bodies, nightmares had plagued her ever since their brutal murders. A man had been arrested, convicted and sentenced to two life terms, but just recently DNA evidence had proved that man's innocence.

So the real killer was still out there.

It couldn't have been the man Thad had shot. He hadn't been much older than Thad's thirty-one, so he would have been just a kid himself two decades ago. That was about all they knew for certain about the dead guy—his approximate age and that his first name had maybe been Wade.

Even though *Wade* hadn't been old enough

to be the Christmas Eve Killer, as the media had dubbed their parents' murderer, Thad still wanted to learn more about the man he'd killed. Like why he'd been stalking and trying to kill Natalie....

"You used to come into my room and comfort me," she remembered with a wistful sigh.

"And now you're comforting me." He grinned at the irony.

She leaned her head on his shoulder, her blond hair tickling his cheek. He and his oldest brother, Devin, were dark haired and blue eyed like their father had been, while his brother Ash and Natalie had their mother's green eyes. Natalie had her straight blond hair, too.

But her sensitive heart was hers alone. "It's my fault you're having nightmares."

"No, it's not," he denied. She couldn't have guessed what he'd realized—he had been the first to notice the resemblance between her and her stalker.

"Yes, it is, because you had to shoot that man to save me and Gray." She lifted her head and stared up into his face. "I can't imagine how horrible that must have been for you, killing a man. That's why you're having nightmares, Thad."

If killing a man gave him nightmares, then he wouldn't have been able to sleep for the past several years.

"Maybe you need to talk to someone," she suggested, "so that you can sleep. I bet Gray could help you." Love radiated from her at the mention of her fiancé. "He was a Navy SEAL, you know."

"I know." That was why their brother Devin had hired Grayson Scott to protect her when Natalie had first mentioned her stalker to Devin's fiancée, Jolie Carson.

"Or if you're not comfortable talking to Gray, you could talk to Ash." Ash, the second oldest of the Kendall orphans, was also former military and a detective with the St. Louis Police Department.

The oldest, Devin, had joined their uncle, who had become their guardian after their parents' murders, in running their father's communications business. Natalie, the baby at twenty-six, worked for Kendall Communications, too, as a graphic artist in the PR department. Thad was the only Kendall who had left St. Louis and hadn't come back except for very rare visits to check on his family.

Even now he wasn't back for good. Once

his parents' murderer was finally brought to justice, he would leave again.

"Natalie." He squeezed her shoulders. "I don't need to talk to anyone about the shooting." But he needed to talk to someone. The DNA results had to be back by now. But instead of thinking about the crime-scene tech who was now his sister-in-law, another woman came to mind. Hell, that woman had never really left his mind once during the four years since he had seen her last.

"If you don't want to talk to anyone about the shooting, you're not going to want to leave the estate," she said with a glance toward the window. Sunlight streamed through the partially open blinds.

"Those damn reporters camped out yet?"

She giggled. "You say that like you're not one of them."

He wasn't. But only a very few people knew that. Everyone else believed he was really just an award-winning photojournalist for a cable network. "Well, I'd rather be doing the interviewing," he clarified, "than being interviewed."

"Wouldn't we all," she murmured.

Growing up a Kendall in St. Louis had been like growing up royalty. The media had recorded their lives, snapping pictures at school dances and proms and their high school graduations. And that coverage always intensified this time of year, around the anniversary of their parents' murders. Since the discovery that their killer had never been caught, the media had gone crazy trying to get the siblings' reactions. And in Thad's case, his story about the shooting his first night back in St. Louis.

"Is that why you're here and not at Gray's?" he asked. "You're hiding out?"

Her face flushed with embarrassment. "Hey, we're not married yet."

"Hasn't stopped the two of you from being joined at the hip," he teased, amused that her big brother's knowing that she stayed at her fiancé's would fluster her so much.

"Well, he's my bodyguard," she reminded him. "He's supposed to be with me 24/7."

He chuckled. "Somehow I don't think he considers that a duty of his job. He loves you."

She emitted a happy sigh. "Isn't it wonderful? Devin, Ash and I all found love—true love."

"Yeah, wonderful," he murmured sarcastically.

She pinched his arm. "You're such a cynic. I can't wait until you fall in love, brother dear. You're going to fall the hardest of all of us."

He already had. But that was just one more thing his family didn't know about him. Hell, until he'd left her *he* hadn't even known how hard he'd fallen for her. By the time he'd realized the extent of his feelings, he had been a world away from her and in too deep to get out.

Hell, he hadn't even been able to come back when his family needed him most. By the time he'd finally escaped the life that hardly anyone knew he lived, he'd almost been too late. Natalie had nearly died in the fire her stalker had set to her cottage, and her fiancé had nearly been shot to death trying to save her from that fire. The stalker had ambushed Gray as he'd carried Natalie from her burning cottage.

Thad had absolutely no regrets over killing her stalker. In the same situation, he would not have done anything differently—except for making sure he'd had the kill shot before Gray had taken a bullet for his sister. But his future brother-in-law was fine now, fully recovered. Thad was the one everyone kept looking at like he was going to fall apart. Because none of them knew about his work for the U.S. Department of State, they thought the shooting was bothering him.

What was really bothering him was the fact that his parents' murderer had never paid for his horrific crimes. Thad wanted justice.

But that wasn't all he wanted.

CAROLINE EMERSON CROOKED her neck to cradle the cordless phone between her ear and her shoulder while she folded laundry. Her best friend was given to marathon telephone calls even though they'd just seen each other that morning at church and saw each other every weekday at the elementary school where they both taught.

"You still haven't heard from him?" Tammy asked.

A hard knot tightened in Caroline's stomach, but she forced a smile into her voice. "No."

"But he's been back in St. Louis more than a week now."

And what a week it had been. His handsome face had been all over the news.

Caroline reminded her overly romantic friend, "He's been a little busy."

For once he had been making news instead

of reporting it: *World famous photojournalist who spent years in war-torn countries finds most danger at home, forced to kill to protect his family.*

"I was sure he would call you," Tammy said, her voice heavy with disappointment.

"I was sure he wouldn't." But even though her head had been sensibly convinced that he wouldn't, her stupid heart had held out hope, so she was disappointed, too.

"I set the two of you up four years ago because I knew you were perfect for each other." Because Tammy had found the love of her life, she was convinced that everyone else could find the happiness she had with her husband. She didn't realize how fortunate she had been to find Steve Stehouwer—the sweet man was one in a million.

For the magical month that Thad had been home in St. Louis, Caroline had believed Tammy's matchmaking successful. But she'd had years since then that had proved how wrong her friend had been. Thad Kendall had not been perfect for her at all. But he had given her one perfect…

"He has been busy." Tammy rallied her eternal optimism. "So you should call him."

Caroline choked on her own saliva and the nerves that rushed over her. "No."

"You should have called him right after you found out you were—"

"I couldn't reach him then," Caroline interrupted, "and I doubt I'd be able to reach him now."

"I could see if Steve has a contact at the station who could get a message to him." Steve and Thad had taken a journalism class together in college; that was how Tammy had met and then proceeded to introduce Thad to Caroline.

But Steve was an anchor at a local station whereas Thad traveled the world. He'd only been home a month when they'd been going out. Between assignments, he'd explained. Somehow she hadn't thought he was talking about just photojournalism jobs.

The ever-romantic Tammy had believed he would fall in love with Caroline and stay home. And maybe, for a little while, she had let herself believe that, too. Or at least hope. But those hopes had been dashed forever when he'd left.

As far as Caroline knew, this was the first time he had been home in nearly four years. And in all that time, he hadn't called, hadn't sent her a letter or even a text message. He had obviously forgotten all about her.

BEFORE COMING HERE, Thad had driven all around St. Louis, over the Poplar Street Bridge and under the shadow of the infamous six-hundred-thirty-story-tall Gateway Arch. Sentimentality hadn't inspired his impromptu tour of the city he hadn't seen in years, though.

He had driven all over Greater St. Louis to lose whatever reporters and whoever else might have been following him. So he was certain that his was the only car that turned onto *her* street.

Four years ago she'd lived in an apartment building, close to the elementary school where she taught second grade. She still worked at the same school, but she had moved out of the apartment into a subdivision with cul-de-sacs and a mixture of newer ranch homes and well-maintained older brick Cape Cods. Thad glanced down at the paper on which he'd scribbled her house number, but before he could locate her address, his cell rang.

The distinctive ring belonged to his boss—his *real* boss—not the executive at the network everyone else believed to be his real boss. He answered with a succinct "Kendall."

"We have a problem."

He mentally cursed. "Michaels still hasn't been found?" He shouldn't have left—not with a man missing. But if he hadn't come back when he had…he shuddered to think what would have happened to Natalie and Gray that night.

"He's been found," Agent Anya Smith replied.

His gut tightened with dread. "Not alive?"

"No. And before he died, he'd been tortured. We have no idea what he might have revealed to his captors before his death." That was what she considered the problem.

Thad considered the problem the senseless murder of a good man. "Len Michaels wouldn't have given them any information."

"He had a wife and kids he wanted to get home to," Anya warned. "He would have revealed anything if he thought it might get him back with his family."

Grief and regret tore a ragged sigh from Thad. "His wife lost her husband, his children their father," he reminded his boss.

"He should have gotten out before now,"

Anya said. "Being a family man made him a liability…to the rest of us."

"I don't really believe—"

She obviously didn't care what he thought, as she interrupted him to warn, "He might have given you up, Kendall."

He hadn't worked with Michaels that often. The agent had acted as a translator, and Thad's fluency with languages was too well-known for him to warrant a translator. But their last assignment had taken him to an unfamiliar territory, and so he and Michaels had worked together.

Then Anya had passed on Devin's message to Thad that he was needed back home, and he'd had to leave. Michaels had disappeared shortly after. Guilt twisted Thad's guts. If he hadn't left, maybe Michaels would have made it home to his wife and kids.

"If he did give me up, I'm not sure that I'd blame him," he murmured.

"Kendall, don't beat yourself up about this," his supervisor advised. "I authorized your leaving. I sent in another operative…." Her voice cracked with regret, but then she cleared her throat.

"That operative obviously wasn't as good as I am," he said without conceit. It was simple fact that he'd never lost another operative or a contact.

"You're one of the best," she agreed. "You need to wrap up whatever's going on in St. Louis and get back in the field."

"Soon," he vowed.

His parents' killer had gone free for too long; justice could wait no longer.

"I need you back out there. I don't have to worry about you," she said. "You're not a liability."

"No, you don't have to worry about me," he agreed. He had no wife. No kids.

But he might have…had he not left Caroline. She was the marrying kind; he never should have called her after that first disastrous double date with her friends. But she was so damn beautiful. And it wasn't because of her summer-sky-blue eyes or her silky dark blond hair; it was the kind of beauty that radiated from the inside out. And he'd wanted to see her again and again.

And now, nearly four years after he had left her, he'd wanted to see her again. He clicked off with his boss and then looked up at her house. He didn't need to check the address—he instinctively knew it was hers.

The brick Cape Cod had a giant wreath

on its oak front door. The house sat behind a white picket fence, garlands strung from each snow-topped picket. At night, lights would probably twinkle against the evergreen branches. Lights were also wrapped around the pine tree in the yard and hung like icicles from the eaves.

All the decorations had his stomach churning with his revulsion for Christmas. Caroline loved it, which was just another thing they hadn't had in common, another reason they could have never made a long-term relationship work.

He had often wondered, over the years, if he should have left her. He had fantasized over what they could have had if he'd stayed instead....

A lopsided snowman in the front yard. No, this would have never been his home. Ever since his parents had been murdered in their beds on Christmas Eve, Thad had not had a home, or at least he'd never let any place feel like one.

And Caroline was all about home and hearth. Smoke puffed out of the top of the brick chimney—her house even had a fireplace. She probably had two-point-two children by now and a loving, devoted husband who worked a boring nine-to-five job so that he could be home every night to help her with dinner and the kids' baths.

Thad respected that she had her own life now, and that was why he hadn't given in to his temptation to mine his St. Louis sources for information about her. He'd hoped she had the life she had always wanted and deserved. He needed to just drive away and leave her alone. But instead he shut off his car and stepped out onto the snow-dusted street. Since getting Devin's message, he'd been in hell. How could his parents' killer be free?

But there'd been more, so much more that had happened to his family. His brother Ash had nearly lost his fiancée and their unborn child. Uncle Craig had nearly been framed for his own brother's and sister-in-law's murders. And Natalie, sweet Natalie, had been stalked and terrorized. His family had been through hell.

So Thad needed an angel. As much as he needed to leave her alone, he needed even more to see her face.

She wasn't the one who opened the door at his knock, though. At first it looked as though it had swung open of its own volition, until Thad adjusted his line of vision way down to the little boy who stood in the doorway. With his dark brown hair and blue eyes, the kid was a miniature version of Thad.

Caroline had had his son.

Chapter Two

"Good luck," Tammy whispered through the open driver's window after Caroline had buckled Mark into his booster seat in the back.

"Thank you," Caroline replied. For the good-luck wishes and for picking up her son, so that the little boy wouldn't overhear the explosion that was certain to come from Thad Kendall.

Despite the cold wind that drove icy snowflakes into her face and chin-length hair, Caroline stood outside, watching Tammy's minivan drive away. And avoiding Thad.

But he deserved an explanation, which he'd already agreed to wait for until Tammy picked up Mark, so they could talk in private. She drew in a deep breath, the cold air burning her lungs, and turned back to the house. Through the big picture window, she could see Thad pacing the length of her living room—giving a wide berth around the Christmas tree as if it were a vicious dog that might attack if he got too close.

She pulled open the front door and stepped into the room with him. Warmth from the crackling fire immediately melted the snow-flakes from her hair and skin so that they ran down her face like tears. Her fingers trembled as she brushed away the moisture. Despite the warmth of the room, she kept her coat on, wrapped tight around her as if she still needed the protection.

Thad didn't stop pacing. She remembered how he had never stopped moving. How had he ever managed to hold still long enough to take the poignant photos of war and tragedy that had earned him such accolades in his nearly decadelong career?

"So are you going to try to lie to me?" he asked. His voice, colder even than the winter wind, chilled her to the bone.

"Lie to you?" she repeated, the question echoing hollowly off the coffered ceiling.

"Play me for a fool, deny that that little boy is my son," he said, heat in his voice now as his blue eyes burned with anger.

Still, she shivered. "Mark is definitely your son."

"Then why did you keep that from me?" he demanded to know with an intensity that might have had Caroline taking a step back if righteous indignation wasn't pumping through her veins right now.

Except for on the news and in newspapers, she hadn't seen him in nearly four years. Her anger ignited and she lashed out, "How was I supposed to tell you? When you called me? When you wrote me? Oh, yeah, you didn't do any of those things!"

He shoved his hand through his hair, tousling the dark brown strands. "We agreed that a clean break would be easier."

"I agreed." As she'd fought back her tears and silently called herself all kinds of a fool for falling for him when he'd been clear right from the start that he had to leave again. Why hadn't she listened to him instead of Tammy and her own stupid heart? "But the clean break was your idea, so I figured you wanted nothing to do with me anymore."

"Caroline…" He reached out but pulled his hand back before touching her face. "I never led you on. I was straight with you up front."

And that was why she should have never

gone out with him. But the attraction between them had been so strong—as strong
as it was now, her skin tingling even though
he hadn't touched her—that she hadn't been
able to resist. And she really had hoped that
her friend was right, that if he fell in love
with her, he would stay.

But he hadn't....

"I know you had to leave," she said, and
she suspected she even knew why—because
it was too hard for him to stay in the city
where his parents had been so brutally murdered. "But I didn't know where you were."

"You could have given a message to my
brothers Devin or Ash or to my uncle Craig,"
he said. "They would have made sure I got
it."

She laughed, but with bitterness not amusement. "I don't know your brothers or your
uncle. I never met your family," she reminded
him, feeling now as she had then, as if she
had been some dirty secret of his. Had dating
an elementary school teacher been so far beneath the status of one of the illustrious Kendalls of St. Louis that he'd been embarrassed
to introduce her to his family?

"But you know who they are and how to
reach them," he stubbornly persisted.

Of course she knew; everyone in St. Louis and most of the United States knew who every one of the Kendalls was.

"But your family doesn't know who *I* am," she retorted. "What reason would they have to believe that I was really carrying your child and not just trying to make a claim on the Kendall fortune?"

According to local gossip, several other women had tried to get their hands on some Kendall money albeit through his brothers and not Thad.

"My brothers or uncle would have told me that you'd come to see them—"

"When?" she interrupted. "Are you in regular contact with them? Have you even come home in the past four years?" She waited, almost hoping he hadn't so she wouldn't be disappointed that he hadn't contacted her earlier.

"I would have gotten word," he insisted, a muscle twitching along his tightly clenched jaw.

"And what would you have done?" she wondered. "Would you have come back home? Would you have given up your nomad lifestyle for diaper duty and two-a.m. feedings?"

"You did that all alone?" He glanced around the living room as if he were looking for her support system.

Her parents had moved to Arizona years ago, coming back to St. Louis for only a few weeks every summer. Except for her friends, she had no one.

She nodded in response, but she didn't want his sympathy or his guilt. "And I loved every minute of it. Mark was the easiest baby and now he's the sweetest little boy."

"I guess I will have to take your word for what kind of baby he was since I've missed out on those years," he said.

He had stopped his restless pacing and stood now in front of the portrait wall of her living room, staring wistfully at all the pictures of their son. In addition to the studio portraits she'd had taken every few months, she'd framed collages of snapshots, too. She'd recorded every special moment in his life, and hers, because she'd been there. Thad hadn't. Maybe he wouldn't have been even if he'd known. But she'd robbed him of that choice.

Now the guilt was hers. She should have tried to talk to his family so that one of them might have gotten word to him. It hadn't been fair of her to just assume that he wouldn't have wanted any involvement in his son's life just because he hadn't wanted any involvement in hers.

"But I don't intend to miss out on anything else, Caroline," Thad said, his voice low and deep as if he were issuing a threat. "I am going to be part of his life."

"For how long?" she asked. "Just long enough to break his heart when you leave again?" Just like he had broken hers.

THAD'S HEAD POUNDED, tension throbbing at his temples and at the base of his skull. Maybe it was the chemicals in his new sister-in-law's crime lab at the St. Louis Police Department that had caused the headache.

But the fumes weren't toxic or Rachel wouldn't have been working still, not in her condition. The petite brunette was very pregnant, her belly protruding through the sides of the white lab coat.

What had Caroline looked like when she was pregnant? She was taller than Rachel with more generous curves. Had she hidden her pregnancy for a while? Being a single mom might have caused her problems at the elementary school where she worked.

He hadn't asked about that. He'd been too stunned and angry to do more than yell at her. And he hadn't talked to his son at all. Knowing how close he'd been to losing his temper, he had let her call her friend to pick up the boy. Instead of talking to him while they waited, Thad had just stared at the kid and had probably scared him.

Had he scared Caroline, too? After he'd demanded a relationship with his son, she had asked him to leave, saying that she needed time to think. That had been a couple of days ago.

All he'd been doing was thinking.

"Hey, little bro!" Devin snapped his fingers in Thad's face. "You called this meeting. Down here." The CEO of Kendall Communications glanced around the sterile lab and shuddered. "What's going on?"

"I don't care," Ash murmured as he pressed a kiss against the nape of Rachel's neck, which her high ponytail left exposed. "He gave me an excuse to see my gorgeous wife."

"Get a room," Thad grumbled.

"You're just jealous," Ash teased. But he was also right.

Thad was jealous that he'd missed out on seeing Caroline like Rachel was now, glow-ing and beautiful in her pregnancy...with his son.

The door to the lab opened again. "I'm here," a deep voice murmured as former navy SEAL Grayson Scott joined them. "And if my fiancée asks, I was out bonding with my brothers-in-law-to-be."

"How are we bonding?" Devin asked with a grin. His eyes gleamed with curiosity and mischief. "Drinking? Working out?"

Color flushed Gray's face, and he grumbled his reply. "We're Christmas shopping."

Rachel laughed. "Now you're going to have to actually go shopping, so that you weren't really lying to Natalie."

The thought of Christmas shopping, of the music and the crowds and all the goddamn cheer, had Thad's stomach churning.

"It's better that she doesn't know why we're all together," Thad pointed out. "There is no point in upsetting Natalie until we know the truth."

Rachel nodded and was suddenly all business. "The FBI lab results came back." She stared at Thad, her hazel eyes narrowed with suspicion. "I don't know how you got the results rushed, but the DNA report is back already. It confirms my findings."

Thad hadn't needed a DNA test to prove that he was Mark's father. The little boy was him twenty-eight years ago.

"So was I right?"

Rachel studied him again. "I don't know how you knew…."

He shrugged. "I didn't know for sure. But the eyes…" He shuddered even now, thinking of how looking into the dead man's eyes had been like looking into his sister's. Only the color had been different. "So Natalie is only our half sister?"

"According to the DNA tests you all took in comparison to Natalie's samples that you had taken while she was in the hospital, and the dead man's samples I took from the morgue—" Rachel's ponytail bobbed as she nodded "—her stalker was her half brother."

"So she had a different father from all of you?" Gray asked, looking somewhat ill.

"That's the most likely scenario," Devin said with a weary sigh of resignation, as if this was merely confirmation of something he had already suspected.

He'd been older than the rest of them, sixteen, when their parents had been murdered. He remembered them best. Or perhaps, *worst*.

"We need to tell her," Gray said. After

dragging in a deep breath, he added, "*I* need to tell her."

"No," Thad said with a head shake that only intensified the throbbing pain. "I'll tell her."

Gray's jaw clenched. "Any particular reason you want to be the one to tell her?"

Over the years, Thad, Devin and Ash had given Natalie's boyfriends a tough time because none of them had ever been good enough for her. Until now. Grayson Scott was a good man, but that hadn't stopped them all from being a little rough on him in the beginning. He'd had to prove to them, as well as Natalie, how much he loved her. Taking a bullet to save her life had pretty much sealed the deal for all of them.

"I'm the one who killed him," Thad offered in explanation. "I'm the reason she'll never get to know this guy."

"He didn't want to get to know her," Gray reminded him. "He wanted to kill her."

"Why?" Devin asked. "Knowing now that they're related, it makes even less sense that he was stalking her."

"Did you find out anything else from his DNA?" Ash asked his wife. "Like who the hell he is?"

She shook her head. "We already ran his prints. While they matched the ones from the break-in at my apartment, he wasn't in the system."

"So he is the guy who tried to get the DNA results from our parents' crime scene?" Devin asked. "He's the one who tried to destroy the evidence that cleared Rick Campbell?"

The petty thief had been in the wrong place at the wrong time and had done twenty years' time for someone else's crime. He never got the chance to enjoy freedom again. He'd been killed to cover up the corruption that had rushed his conviction in order to clear a high-profile case and advance a career.

Ash gave a grim nod in response to his older brother's question. Rachel had been hurt during the break-in; it was how he had learned she was pregnant since they'd broken up months earlier.

"We need to find out this guy's identity," Gray said. "I'm not even sure Wade is his real first name. It's just what he told the girl at the coffee shop Natalie goes to."

"Did you get any leads from the photograph that was released to the media?" Devin asked Ash.

Ash shook his head. "The new chief wouldn't let us release the morgue photo, and that surveillance photo from the ATM camera outside the coffee shop is too grainy for anyone to make a positive identification."

Devin turned to Thad. "Why don't you leak a better photo?"

"The chief will know where the photo came from," Rachel warned them.

"We don't need to know who this guy was," Thad said, which elicited gasps from his family.

Gray's neck snapped back in indignation. "What the hell—he tried to kill Natalie—"

"He's dead now. He's no longer a threat," Thad pointed out. "He was about my age. He couldn't have been our parents' killer."

"Our parents' killer might not be out there anymore," Ash remarked. "He could be locked up or dead. But *this guy,* Natalie's half brother, is the one who attacked Rachel to try to destroy the DNA evidence from our parents' murder—"

"Why did he do it? He couldn't have been their killer," he repeated, "so he must have been trying to protect someone."

Gray sucked in a breath. "Maybe that's why he tried to kill Natalie."

"Because she did see something that night our parents were murdered," Ash said. "Maybe the killer…"

"We don't need to know who this Wade guy was," Thad repeated, "although finding that out will help us learn what we really need to know—who his father is."

"And if he was locked up or dead, his son wouldn't have gone to the extent he had to protect him," Ash reasoned. He wrapped his arms around Rachel, as if he needed to protect her even inside the lab in the basement of the St. Louis Police Department.

Gray swore beneath his breath. "So even though that son of a bitch is dead, there's still a threat out there?"

Thad shrugged. "I don't know for sure. Rachel, we'll need you to run the DNA from the old crime scene and compare it to the stalker's DNA."

Her brow furrowed. "I don't have access to any of the original evidence anymore," she said, patting her belly. "Not even the results. I've been taken off the case because no one with any connection to a Kendall is being allowed near the case files or the evidence."

"They don't trust that we really want justice," Ash said.

"Can you talk to someone with access and have them run it?" Thad persisted.

She shook her head. "The stalker was too young to be considered a viable suspect in the old murders. They won't look at him for any connection."

"That's why the Kendalls should be running the investigation," Thad said. It was why they were going to damn well run their own.

A short while later, when Thad walked through the parking garage to his car, he knew that there was definitely a threat. He felt someone's gaze boring into his back. It could have been reporters, but he doubted it. If they'd made it past the police department parking garage attendant, then they would have been rushing him with cameras and questions. They wouldn't have just watched him.

But then why would the killer watch him? He hadn't witnessed anything the night his parents died. He'd done nothing to save them. But he had saved lives in his real job. He'd also taken lives. Maybe Michaels had given him up. He reached beneath his jacket, but his holster was locked up, with his gun, inside his glove box. He wouldn't have gotten it past the security scanners in the police department unless he'd had Ash clear it for him. And his brother would have had too many questions about Thad having a license for a concealed weapon.

Now, as the hairs on the nape of his neck lifted with foreboding, Thad wished he'd answered those questions, so that he was armed. Keeping close to vehicles for cover, he visually scanned the garage, looking for whoever was staring at him with such intensity. Yes, there was definitely a threat still out there, and it was focused wholly on Thad.

ONE KILLER ALWAYS RECOGNIZES another...

Thad Kendall couldn't see him through the tinted windows of his SUV, but still Ed ducked down when the man turned toward his vehicle. How could anyone be fooled by Kendall's *cover?*

He was so much more than a bored rich kid or a globe-trotting reporter. Sure, maybe it was because of where he'd reported stories that he moved as he did—as if he had a target on his back. But when he'd felt Ed watching him, he had reached for a gun whereas a reporter's instinct would have been to grab a microphone or a camera instead. Not a weapon.

Kendall was also a damn good shot…when he was armed. But he had no gun now. No protection at all. And he was so close. All Ed would have to do was start the engine, stomp on the gas and run him down. Ed shook with anticipation—not withdrawal. He didn't need a drink. He needed vengeance. He could almost imagine the satisfying crunch of the man's bones beneath the tires of his SUV.

It would hurt Kendall. But not enough.…

The son of a bitch wouldn't feel as much pain as he had caused. So killing him wouldn't be satisfying at all—not until Thad Kendall had suffered. All Ed had to do was watch and figure out what would cause Thad the most pain.

Chapter Three

This time Caroline opened the door to his knock. And no one was surprised, like when Mark had let Thad into their house. Then she had been on the phone with Tammy when the doorbell rang, so her son had beaten her to the door and totally disregarded the rule of not opening it unless he knew who was at it.

This time she'd known Thad was coming because she had invited him. But still her heart started beating faster at the sight of him. Fluffy snowflakes melted in his dark hair and clung to his high cheekbones and strong jaw. She stepped back to let him inside, but he hesitated, glancing over his shoulder.

She followed his gaze to the street. Was he waiting for someone? A lawyer? That was why she'd called him—because she hadn't wanted to force him to fight for his parental rights. With the full resources of the Kendall money and power, he couldn't lose.

But she could potentially lose her son. Her salary barely stretched to cover her mortgage, Mark's day care and their living expenses. She couldn't afford a lawyer, too.

Thad finally stepped inside and closed the door, shutting out the snow and the cold and whoever he might have been looking for.

"Is Mark here?" he asked, glancing around the inside of the house like he had the outside.

Was that a habit he'd picked up from traveling to war-torn countries? He'd probably had to learn to be vigilant in order to stay alive. A lot of reporters hadn't made it back from the places Thad had been.

Caroline drew in a shaky breath. "Mark is upstairs."

"So you're not worried about him hearing us fight?" he asked with a glance toward the open stairwell.

"I'm not going to fight you."

"What does that mean?" he asked. His eyes, which were the same sapphire-blue of his son's, widened in surprise. "You're going to let me see him?"

Her stomach tightened with nerves, but she couldn't deny her son the chance to get to know his father. Given Thad's lifestyle, this could possibly be the only chance the boy would ever get. Too bad he would probably be too young to remember him. "If that's what you really want…"

"He's my son. Of course I want to see him," he replied, as if offended by her suggestion. "I've already missed so much."

"And you'll miss even more when you leave again."

He ducked his chin as if she'd taken a swing at him. But he didn't deny that he would leave. "I have a job to do."

"You don't have to leave St. Louis to be a reporter," she pointed out. "You could get a job at any station or paper in the city."

"Not *reporting* the story," he said. "In St. Louis, I would *be* the story."

"Because of the shooting."

Everyone else had been so surprised that Thad Kendall had killed a man. Everyone but Caroline. Beneath his charm and devastating grin, there was a ruthlessness that she had glimpsed the day he'd left her without even a backward glance.

He had a single-minded intensity about his job that seemed to be about more than achieving success or fame. She suspected there was

much more to Thad Kendall than anyone realized.

And he was her son's father. She swallowed
a sigh.

"You're not looking at me like everyone
else has been," he said. He was actually the
one looking at her, his gaze intent on her face.

"How's that?" She had barely let herself
look at him at all, as she was determined to
not let her foolish heart rule her head once
again. She would not fall for Thad Kendall,
no matter how damn handsome he was.

"All my family," he said, "even members of
the press keep looking at me like I'm going
to fall apart because I pulled the trigger and
killed a man."

"I think you've had to do a lot harder
things than that in your life," she admitted.

He jerked his head in a grim nod. Then he
stepped closer and skimmed his fingers along
her jaw. "Leaving you was one of the hardest."

She sucked in a breath as her traitorous
heart slammed against her ribs. "Don't." She
moved back so that his hand fell away from
her face. "Just don't…"

"It's true."

"You left and never looked back," she reminded him. "I'm not looking back, either. I'm looking ahead to when you leave again and I have to explain to Mark."

"I'll explain to Mark that it's my job to go to other countries."

"Will you want to make a clean break with him, too?" She'd worried about that for the past few sleepless nights since her son had opened the door to his father. Mark had had so many questions about the stranger who'd come to their house, and he had deserved to know the truth.

"No. I'll stay in contact with him," he promised as he stepped closer again. His voice dropped to an intimate murmur. "And with you…"

His lips curved into that devastating grin. He was arrogant—he couldn't look like he did and not realize how women wanted him. And he was a Kendall, used to getting what he wanted, and apparently since he was back in St. Louis, he wanted her.

With an effort she steadied her racing pulse and shook her head. "I don't want a relationship with you."

His grin faded. "Caroline…"

"Truthfully, I don't want you to have a relationship with Mark," she said, keeping her voice low so that her son wouldn't overhear. "I'm afraid you're going to break his heart like you did mine."

He groaned. "I never meant to hurt you."

"I know," she admitted. "And you won't mean to hurt him, either. But you will."

"So what do you want me to do?" he asked. "Pretend that I never saw him? That I don't know I have a son? Do you want me to just walk away?"

That was the problem. She didn't want him to walk away. Ever. But he would. "It's what you do best."

"Damn it! You're not being fair!"

"No. I'm not," she readily agreed. But she needed to keep reminding herself that she couldn't fall for him again. She wouldn't be able to help heal her son's broken heart if she was dealing with her own.

"I didn't know how much I hurt you," he said. "I'm sorry."

She shook her head, refusing his apology. "I'm over you," she said, trying to convince them both of that. "And I intend to *stay* over you."

"If you're so over me, why haven't you moved on?" he challenged her. "Why aren't you married or involved with someone else?"

"How—how do you know that I'm not involved with someone?" she asked.

"Since finding out about Mark, I checked with some of my sources...."

Damn Tammy. "I'm focused on my son right now," she said, "not dating."

"I can't believe men haven't been beating down your door to take you out," he said.

She laughed at the outrageous compliment, refusing to be charmed again. Mark was three and a half, but she had fifteen pounds of baby weight to lose yet. Maybe twenty.

"You're beautiful," he said. "Even more beautiful now than you were four years ago."

Her stomach muscles tightened with desire, but she shook her head. "I am smarter now than I was four years ago. I'm not going to fall for your patented Kendall charm."

"Patented?"

"Already at three, Mark has it. He can wrap me completely around his little finger." Just like Thad used to be able to do.

"You're not immune to me," he said, his voice husky and his eyes bright with desire. "And I can prove it to you."

When she opened her mouth to ask him how, his lips were there covering hers. His tongue delved deep, stroking over hers, stroking her passion from flickering flame to full conflagration. He'd wrapped his arms around her, too, so that she couldn't step back. But she didn't want to get away; she wanted to get closer. His chest pressed against hers, his heart beating the same frantic rhythm as hers.

"Hey!" exclaimed a little voice, full of curiosity. "What are you doing to my mommy?"

They broke apart as guiltily as teenagers caught necking on the couch. Caroline would have laughed at the shock on Thad's flushed face if she hadn't felt more like crying. She didn't know what was bringing her closer to tears—the kiss or the fact that her son had interrupted it.

THAD'S SKIN BURNED, his fingers numb from the cold as he rolled a snowball across Caroline's front yard. He'd brought no gloves with him and Caroline's were too small. But when Mark had asked him to build another snowman to go with the lopsided one already in their front yard, Thad had been unable to refuse no matter how many excuses he'd had to do just that.

She was right. The kid had the Kendall charm but with Caroline's innate kindness and generosity.

"I can roll it," Mark said, putting his mittened hands over Thad's. "You're cold."

Maybe his skin was cold, but the rest of him was still on fire from kissing Caroline. If Mark hadn't interrupted them…

Caroline probably would have pulled away. She was over him. He'd kissed her to prove her wrong, but instead he'd proved to himself that he wasn't over her. Not even close.

He wanted more than a kiss, but she wanted nothing from him but for him to not hurt their son. He stared at the tiny, mittened hands clasping his, and his heart twisted in his chest.

"Just a li'l bigger," the boy directed. When the snowball grew to the size of a beach ball, he stopped and tried to lift it.

Thad lifted it instead, setting it atop the other two balls they'd formed into the base of the snowman. The lopsided snowman was actually a snow lady, and he and Mark had already made a snow boy. "There. It's done."

Mark shook his head. "We gotta make his face." He reached in his pocket for the things that Caroline had given him after she'd bundled him into a snowsuit, boots, mittens, scarf and hat.

She was a great mom, just as he'd known

she would be. That was another reason he'd forced himself to leave her four years ago. She'd deserved more than he was capable of giving. Because of his real job, he'd never intended to be a husband or a father. He hadn't wanted to leave a family behind like Len Michaels had.

But he had left behind a son...without ever realizing he'd become a father.

"Here," Mark said, shoving a carrot into Thad's cold hand. "You're gonna have to put it on 'cuz I'm not big enough."

Thad handed back the carrot and then, his hands shaking slightly, he slid them around his son and lifted him onto his shoulders. "You're big enough now."

A giggle slipped from Mark's lips. "I'm too big now." He wrapped one arm around Thad's neck and leaned forward to reach their snowman. His tongue sticking out between his lips in concentration, he carefully arranged the carrot and a collection of colored stones to make the snowman's face, which he must have been comparing to Thad's because he kept looking back and forth between them.

"Mommy says these rocks are the same color as my eyes," he remarked. He turned toward Thad. "They're the same color as yours, too."

"You look like me when I was a little boy," Thad said.

After discovering he had a son, he'd found some of the old photo albums his aunt Angela kept in the library, and he'd flipped through the pictures of himself and his family. He hadn't looked through the albums in years because he hadn't wanted to see old pictures of his parents. Surprisingly there hadn't been as many in the albums as he'd thought there would have been. The photos had mostly been of just him and his brothers and some of Natalie.

He lifted Mark from his shoulders and then crouched down to the boy's level. "Do you know why you look like me?"

The child gave a solemn nod. "'Cuz you're my dad."

Thad sucked in a breath of surprise. "You know?" Kissing Caroline had distracted him so much that he hadn't known whether the boy actually knew who he was yet or not. Mark hadn't said anything to Thad but to wonder what he'd been doing to his mother and then to ask him to make a snowman with him.

"When I came home from Aunt Tammy and Uncle Steve's, Mommy told me who you are," he said, as if it had been no big deal for his father to finally show up after three years.

"Do you have any questions for me?" Thad said. He had a million for Mark. He wanted to learn everything about the little boy, everything that he had missed.

Mark shook his head, though, and returned his attention to the cluster of snowmen. "Look!" he exclaimed with pride. "There's a snow mommy and a snow kid and now a snow daddy."

"Wow," Thad said, trying to sound suitably impressed. This meant a lot to his son.

"We have a snow family," Mark said with a bright smile of satisfaction, as if a family was something he'd wanted for a while.

Thad stood back to admire the family, but then the sound of an idling engine drew his gaze to the street beyond the picket fence. Had the white SUV followed him again?

He suspected it had been in the parking garage the day before when he'd felt someone watching him. Then he'd thought he glimpsed it near the estate, as well. But he'd made sure he wasn't followed here, taking a circuitous route again.

And really he was probably overreacting. There were a million white SUVs. He hadn't noted the plate, so he couldn't be certain if the one he'd seen near the estate was the same one or even the same make and year as the one from the parking garage.

But he couldn't shake the uneasiness he'd felt in the parking garage, the sense of fore-boding that someone was watching him with an intense hatred. He glanced toward the house and confirmed that he was being watched.

Caroline stood at the living-room window, staring intently at him. He doubted she was reliving that kiss as he had and wishing they hadn't been interrupted. He suspected instead that she was watching to make sure that he hadn't already screwed up with Mark.

She was right to worry about his parenting skills. The only parenting he'd ever really known had been when Uncle Craig and Aunt Angela became his and his brothers' and sister's guardians. But that had been a long time ago.

Where he'd been the past several years had had nothing to do with family and everything to do with survival. His own and all those he'd been able to save. He had to go back to finish his assignment and make sure Michaels's killers were brought to justice. But what kind of father could he be to Mark if he wasn't even around?

Something struck the back of his head and exploded in shards of ice that ran down his neck and inside his collar. Thad whirled around so quickly that Mark shrieked and ran from him. He'd stayed alive for years in the most dangerous places in the world but had taken one in the head from his own kid.

He grabbed up a handful of snow and gave chase.

CAROLINE GIGGLED, echoing her son's laughter that she could hear even through the double panes of glass. He'd nailed his father with that snowball. Thad threw a couple at him, careful to miss wide while stepping squarely in front of the ones that Mark threw back at him.

He had no hat, no gloves, not even a scarf, but he didn't seem to care about the cold. The only thing he seemed preoccupied with was the street, as he kept glancing back at it.

Was he expecting someone or was it just a habit for him to constantly survey his surroundings? He hadn't seen that snowball coming.

Just like she hadn't seen his kiss coming. Or maybe she had but she'd wanted it too much to push him away. If Mark hadn't interrupted them, she wouldn't have stopped Thad. Being back in his arms, kissing him, had felt too good—too right. She touched her lips, which tingled yet from the contact with his. She could taste him, too, from when he'd slid his tongue between her lips deep into her mouth.

But she'd meant what she'd told him. Not about being over him—that had been a lie that he'd easily disproved. But about not wanting a relationship with him.

He was her son's father, and that was all he would ever be to her. Not her lover. Not her boyfriend. Not even her friend.

Because she couldn't trust him. But she wouldn't have been able to beat him, either, if she'd fought to keep him away from Mark. Now, seeing them chase each other around the yard, she was glad that she hadn't tried. She'd worked hard the past three years to be both mother and father to her son, but the little boy needed more than she had been able to give him.

He needed Thad.

And, as Thad grinned and laughed, she

began to wonder if Thad didn't need Mark, too. Enough to stay?

But then he glanced to the street again, his body tensing as if he'd identified a threat. To himself or to their son?

She knew when he left St. Louis that Thad put himself in danger. But she hadn't realized until now that he could be in danger in St. Louis, as well. He had killed his sister's stalker, but maybe in doing so, he had picked up his own. Or he had brought danger back with him from one of those war-torn countries?

She'd already had her doubts, but now she was certain that Thad Kendall was more than just a photojournalist.

Whatever else he was, he was also a father now. Would he put their son in the danger that he had constantly put himself in?

Chapter Four

Thad paced his brother's office at Kendall Communications. This was all Devin had ever wanted, to be CEO and take over the running of their father's company.

Uncle Craig might have been technically in charge ever since Joseph Kendall's murder, but the business had grown even more after Devin had joined the company. The stock each of the Kendall siblings had inherited had definitely increased in value due to Devin's initiatives.

Over the years, throughout his travels, Thad had come up with some ideas he'd love to see the company explore. While it may have been just a cover, he had become an expert on communications, some less legal than others.

Devin opened his office door but didn't see Thad yet as he continued his conversation with the red-haired secretary who was also his fiancée. "I didn't give you a chance to give me my messages," he murmured to her as he wiped her lipstick from his mouth. "Did Turner call back?"

"No," she replied. "According to his staff, he hasn't been in the office at all this week and not much in the past few months. Not since his wife died. Maybe he is ready to retire and sell the company."

Turner Connections LLC? Excitement coursed through Thad at the thought of Kendall Communications acquiring the company, which had a good number of defense contracts.

Devin snorted. "He's younger than Uncle Craig. I doubt he's ready to retire."

Jolie sighed. "So you're going to be one of those guys who never knows when to quit…."

"I thought that's what you liked about me…." He leaned forward and kissed her again.

Thad cleared his throat to make them finally aware of his presence.

Jolie pulled free of Devin's arms, her face flaming nearly as red as her hair. "I forgot to tell you Thad was waiting for you."

"Probably because the two of you were too

busy making out to remember I was back here," Thad teased.

Jolie's ringing phone drew her back to the outer office. With only a wave at Thad, she closed the door, leaving him and Devin alone together. Her fiancé stared after her for a moment, as if he'd not been ready to let her go. Natalie was right that each of his siblings had found true love.

"I'm surprised you manage to get any work done around here."

"We don't have a choice." Devin pushed his hand through his hair as he made his way around his desk and dropped into the chair behind it. "It's been pretty crazy around here since September."

That was when Rick Campbell, the man behind bars for their parents' murders, had been cleared of the crime. It hadn't been long before authorities had been looking at a new prime suspect, though.

"I can't believe that damn D.A. tried to blame Uncle Craig." Thad wished he'd been home then; he would have skewered the man in the media. Instead, his family had been smeared. One of the first things he'd noticed on his return was how much his aunt and uncle had aged since he'd been gone. He suspected most of that had happened since September.

"He's a son of a bitch," Devin bitterly murmured. "But clearing Uncle Craig hasn't ended the media circus."

"Some good things came out of the coverage," Thad reminded his older brother.

To protect Jolie's reputation and the company image, Devin had proposed a fake engagement with his secretary. But that engagement had quickly become real when his stubborn brother had finally realized the depths of his feelings for the amazing woman who'd been his friend and right hand for years.

"It would be nice if the press would give us a break for a while," Devin said, "especially with Christmas coming."

"The media coverage has always been bad around Christmastime," Thad reminded him. "And it's even worse this year."

Devin groaned. "It was going to be bad enough, given the twenty-year anniversary, but then with everything else that's happened, the reporters have been relentless."

Which was why Thad had told no one about Mark and Caroline. He didn't want them being pulled into the media circus that was life as a Kendall. It might make Caroline change her mind about allowing Thad time with the boy, and it would no doubt frighten the child. Sure, his family wouldn't let anything slip to reporters, but they would want to meet his son and that meeting would not go unnoticed by the press.

Thad glanced at his watch; he had a meeting to go to. He couldn't believe he'd agreed to what he had. But then Mark had asked and he doubted he'd be able to deny the kid anything. It was a wonder that Caroline hadn't spoiled the little charmer rotten. But he was a great kid. And kids loved Christmas. At least kids whose parents hadn't been murdered on the holiday.

"Will you actually be here this Christmas?" Devin asked.

Thad shrugged. "Depends on when we catch our parents' killer. Finally finding the real murderer is the only way to stop the media frenzy." His body tensed with anger. "And get justice."

"Is that why you came to my office?" Devin asked. "Have you found out something new?"

"*I* did," Thad said, "when we found out that Natalie is only our half sister. But *you* didn't seem very surprised by the news." News that they hadn't shared with anyone who hadn't been at the meeting at Rachel's lab. Thad had to tell Natalie first, but not only did he dread doing that, he'd also been too busy with Mark and Caroline.

Devin leaned back in his chair and rubbed his hand over his face. He had always looked the most like their father but never more so than now. Despite the happiness he'd found with his fiancée, he looked tired and tense, as if he'd been working too hard. At the family company or at keeping family secrets?

"What do you know about that night?" Thad wondered.

"I wasn't even home," Devin reminded him, his voice gruff with guilt. "I'd snuck out."

"You were sixteen," Thad said. "You wanted to hang out with your friends like other sixteen-year-olds. None of what happened was your fault. You couldn't have prevented their deaths if you'd been home."

Knowing Devin, he probably would have gotten himself killed, as well, if he'd even heard anything at all. The master bedroom was in an entirely separate wing of the house from where the kids' bedrooms were, accessed by separate stairwells.

"We'll never know that for certain," Devin pointed out. "But Jolie's helped me deal with it so that I could finally let the past go."

Thad wouldn't be able to do that until the killer had finally been brought to justice, and he wasn't sure that even that would be enough for him. But he wouldn't know until the killer was caught. "What do you know about the past that made Natalie's paternity no surprise to you?"

Devin sighed wearily. "You're not going to let this go. Damn reporter..."

Thad grinned. "That's what I am."

His brother fixed him with a steady gaze as if trying to determine if Thad told him the truth. "Is that all you are?"

Nerves tightened his stomach, but he forced a laugh. "You're not getting out of this." Nor was he getting the truth from Thad. At least not the whole truth. For the most part, he was a real photojournalist, reporting real stories for a real news station, but that was only a small part of what he was.

"I'm not an eleven-year-old kid, Devin. You don't need to protect me anymore. Tell me everything you know about our parents. It's the only way we're going to catch their real killer."

Devin hesitated as if determined to protect their memory.

"I don't remember that much about them," Thad said with regret and guilt. He had been eleven when they'd died; he should have had more memories of them.

What would Mark have when Thad left? At three, would he remember his father at all if, like Michaels, Thad didn't make it out of his next assignment?

"I even looked through old photo albums the other day," he said, but that had been to compare how much his son looked like he had at that age, "and they were hardly in them."

"They weren't around much," Devin admitted. "Dad was here all the time, building this company. He was so ambitious." He surveyed the office with pride in their father's accomplishments.

He needed to take pride in what he'd accomplished, too. But there was something else he'd left out. "What about Mom?" Thad asked.

"You must remember how beautiful she was?"

Thad shrugged. "I don't know if it's my memory, though, or all the news reports that have been done about her over the years. They talk about her like she was a movie star or a princess."

"She was the perfect trophy wife for a rich and powerful man like our father," Devin said. "But she craved attention and always had to be the center of it."

Thad stilled his usual restless pacing and focused on his brother. "What are you saying?"

"I'm saying that they weren't happy."

Thad remembered yelling. Screaming. Slamming doors. And he winced, realizing now what had been happening. "You were the oldest. You knew what was really going on with them."

Devin nodded. "*Affairs*. While Dad was working so hard building this company, Mom was sleeping around."

"With who?" His gut churned at the prospect that there was more than one. Finding Natalie's biological father might not be as easy as Thad had hoped.

"I don't know." Devin shrugged. "I didn't really want to know." He sighed. "Hell, I don't think our father wanted to know, either.

They fought about her going out all the time, but I don't think he realized she'd actually taken it as far as she had—to a hotel one of my friends worked at. Or maybe Dad was just too proud to admit it."

"We need to find out who these men were," Thad said, although the thought of delving into their mother's affairs made him nauseous. There had been no mention of her affairs in the police report. The detectives had figured the murders were the result of a botched burglary and hadn't looked any further for motives or suspects than the man who'd spent twenty years in prison for crimes he hadn't committed.

"Do you remember the name of the hotel?"

Devin named one renowned for its discretion. "That was twenty years ago. You aren't going to find out anything now."

"I'll try." But he didn't like his chances, either.

"That's your theory here?" Devin said. "That Natalie's real dad murdered our parents?"

"Why else would his son try to destroy the evidence that cleared Rick Campbell of the crimes?" he asked. "It's a lead. About the only one we have right now."

"You've been scarce lately," Devin remarked. "Have you been chasing down leads?"

No. He'd been chasing down a squealing little boy who'd thrown snowballs at him. And kissing a woman he'd had no business kissing. After he'd forced that kiss on her, he'd been lucky she hadn't thrown him out. Instead, she'd been accommodating about Thad spending time with their son. But usually she made herself scarce, going grocery shopping or Christmas shopping while he and Mark hung out.

He would spend tonight with both of them, as if they were a real family. But that they could never be, not just because of Thad's real job but because of his real past.

HE WASN'T GOING TO SHOW. Caroline had known it the minute Mark had asked his father to meet them at the mall this Friday night to see Santa. Thad Kendall had been hunkered down, deeply embedded, in war zones. He had nearly been blown up and had almost been abducted, if there was any truth to news reports about him. But Mark asking him to visit Santa Claus was the first time Caroline had ever seen a flicker of panic in his blue eyes.

He hated Christmas. She understood why. And if she didn't have a son who loved it, she would have been more sensitive to Thad's predicament. But she hadn't made an excuse to get him off the hook with Mark. She'd waited for him to come up with his own excuse.

Instead, he'd agreed, with a grim determination, as if he really intended to show up. And maybe he would. Maybe he hadn't lied to their son.

Mark, hanging tight to her hand, glanced around the crowded mall. At his height, there was no way he could see beyond the crush of bodies in the shopping mob scene.

"Where is—" his voice grew soft with wonder "—my daddy?"

The words clutched at Caroline's heart. Daddy. Mark hadn't ever asked very many questions about his father before, probably because he'd seemed to lose interest when she'd said that the man lived in another country and he wouldn't be able to meet him. And Mark hadn't ever acted as if he'd missed having a dad. But now that he knew Thad was his father, his *daddy* was all he ever talked about.

Wishing she could still be enough for him, she crouched down to her son's level. "He's really busy, honey."

Thad hadn't specifically told her, probably because she avoided conversations with him, but she suspected that he was personally trying to find his parents' murderer.

"Something might have come up that he had to deal with," she added. A lead that he was compelled to chase down, as he had chased down so many others in his career.

"But he said he'd meet us here," Mark reminded her, his bottom lip sticking out in a slight pout. Her son never pouted; he was too sweet-natured for petulance. But, as she knew too well, Thad had a way of making a person want more than they ever had before.

"And he might come yet," Caroline said, even though she doubted Thad would show. "But the line for Santa keeps getting longer, so we better get in it before we're so far back we don't get to see him tonight."

The mall stayed open later during the holiday season, but to accommodate the entire line, it would probably have to stay open all night.

"But we're s'pose to meet my daddy by the merry-go-round."

The carousel spun around behind them, Christmas lights twinkling from it and Christmas music blaring out of its speakers. The line for Santa started near it and stretched to the North Pole at the other end of the mall.

"He'll see us," Caroline promised. It wasn't as if the line actually appeared to be moving. The Friday-night crowd of teenagers and shoppers was so thick that people were barely able to move at all. Despite the heat from the crush of bodies, Caroline shivered as an uneasy sensation overcame her.

Maybe she'd picked up Thad's unsettling habit, because she glanced around, trying to figure out what had precipitated her shudder of foreboding. Was someone watching her and Mark?

She didn't notice anyone paying her and her son any particular attention. The other mothers and parents were struggling with their impatient children. The teenagers were more interested in each other, pawing at each other's pockets or holding hands. And the shoppers were focused on trying to make their way through the crowd in order to track down the next items on their lists.

Apparently, she had just picked up Thad's paranoia. At least he had a reason to be paranoid after all those years he'd spent in war zones. The most exciting thing that had ever happened in her life was *Thad*.

Maybe that was why it had been so hard for her to get over him. So hard that, with a flash of guilt, she acknowledged that she didn't really want him to show up at the mall. The less she saw of Thad's handsome face and rock-hard muscular body, the less she had to fight the attraction to him that had only grown more powerful in his four-year absence from her life.

She was so not over him.

Mark tugged at her hand, bringing her attention back to the only man she really needed in her life: her little man. "Your phone's ringing."

The jingle bells music playing from the carousel had an echo inside her purse from her Christmas ringtone. She fumbled inside for her cell and pulled it out. The number on the ID screen was unfamiliar. Maybe Thad?

"Hello?"

She could hear no voice on the other end. "Hello? Is anyone there?"

Static or something emanated from the phone, but the music and crowd noise drowned it out.

"I can't hear you," she said, then tugged on Mark's hand to pull him from the line. "We need to go someplace quieter, so I can hear who's on the phone," she told her son.

"I don't wanna lose my place for Santa," he said, though just a minute ago he hadn't wanted to even get in line without Thad.

"But this could be your daddy." If only she could hear....

"I'll stay right here," Mark promised.

More static emanated from the cell as someone tried to talk to her.

"Hold, please," she implored the caller. "Let me get someplace quieter."

She tugged again on her son's hand, but he resisted her efforts to move him. "Please, Mommy. I wanna see Santa."

She glanced at the line, which was hardly moving except that it was much longer now, circling around behind them. With a sigh, she let go of his hand. "Stay right there," she ordered him. "I'll just step back until I can hear."

But the music from the carousel was so

loud that she had to step back a few paces before she could hear anything beyond jingle bells. She kept her gaze on Mark, though, where he stood between a mom holding a toddler and a trio of probably ten-year-olds. He looked so small. She waved at him, and he waved back.

"Hello?" she said into the phone again.

But now there was no sound, static or otherwise.

"Thad, is that you?"

The line clicked off.

She held out the phone, so that she could call back the number and find out if it had been Thad calling. Mark was going to be so disappointed if he didn't show up. Before she clicked the redial button, she glanced back toward the line for Santa.

Her pulse quickened as she didn't immediately see Mark. Had the line moved? She saw the mom with the toddler and the trio of ten-year-olds standing where they'd been. But Mark was no longer between them. Her heart slammed against her ribs as fear overtook her. Pushing people aside, she ran toward the line.

"Where did the little boy go?" she asked the woman with the toddler.

The lady glanced down as if just realizing that he was gone. "He's not with you?"

Tears stinging her eyes, Caroline shook her head. She grabbed the shoulder of one of the older kids. "Did you see my son?"

The kid stared up at her.

"The little boy who was standing behind you in line," she clarified.

The kid glanced back and shrugged. "I didn't notice him."

She turned to his friends. "Did either of you see where he went?"

Both kids stared at her like she was crazy and then finally shook their heads.

Where had he gone?

Fear choking her, she could barely manage to whisper his name. "Mark…" Then she gathered her courage and yelled, "Mark!"

The music from the carousel drowned out her voice. "Mark!" She pushed through the crowd, frantically searching for him.

Had Thad shown up and taken off with him somewhere? Even though she would be furious with him, she hoped to God that was the case. The Christmas mob was so large that she struggled to push through, let alone find a security guard. She needed to find the information desk. She needed to get help finding her son.

"Mark!" Strong arms grasped her shoulders and spun her around.

"Caroline, what's wrong?"

Relief shuddered through her at the sight of Thad's handsome face, his blue eyes full of concern. "Thank God you're here."

She glanced down, but no little boy stood happily at his daddy's side.

"I'm sorry I'm late," he said.

Panic chased away her momentarily relief. "Where is he?"

"Who?" Thad looked around her, and then his brow furrowed as he realized exactly who was missing.

"Mark," she said, her voice breaking on a sob.

The color drained from his handsome face. "He's not with you...."

"No," she admitted, her voice rising with hysteria "He's gone."

She had spent those sleepless nights worrying about allowing Thad a relationship with their son. She'd been concerned that he would fail as a parent and hurt her sweet baby boy.

But she was the one who'd failed as a parent; she was the one who'd lost their son.

"He's gone…."
His father hadn't taken him.
So who had?

Chapter Five

"I thought it was you on the phone, but I couldn't hear," Caroline said, her voice shaking with fear. "So I backed away from the noise of the carousel. But I kept my eyes on him."

She stared at Thad with eyes that were wide and wet with terror. "I could see him at all times. I only glanced down at the phone for a second. And then he was just…" A sob slipped out of her lips. "Gone."

Thad wrapped his arm around her, holding her close to his side as she relayed the information to him and the security guards he had summoned to search the mall for the missing child.

"We'll find him," he assured her.

Thad had convinced the head of security to lockdown the mall so that no one could leave. Mobs had formed at the doors, protesting the imprisonment. He only hoped it wasn't too late.

"How long ago did you lose sight of him?" he asked. Long enough that someone could have taken their son outside already?

Despite the watch on her wrist, Caroline grabbed her phone from her purse. "Just minutes after the time this call came in."

Thad took the phone from her and noted the time. Because of the throng of shoppers, he had struggled to get through the mall at more than a snail's pace. That was why it had taken him so long to find Caroline—that and his reluctance to even step inside a mall full of Christmas decorations and music.

Guilt and anger at himself gripped him. If only he hadn't acted like such a fool.

His emotions must have shown on his face, because Caroline reassured him now. "We'll find him."

"Whose number is this?" he asked.

She shook her head. "I don't know. I couldn't hear who was talking. I thought it was you, calling to say you weren't going to make it."

He nodded. She'd already said that she hadn't thought he was going to come. When he had promised Mark that he would, he had seen the doubt on her beautiful face. She had thought then that he was lying to their son.

"Was Mark upset that I wasn't here?" he asked, worried that the boy had thrown a tantrum because Thad had been late.

"No."

Now he suspected she was lying.

"He was really anxious that he might not get to see Santa. That's why he didn't want to move out of line when I got the call." Tears streaked down her face. "I never took my eyes off him but for that one second...."

A second was all it took for a bomb to destroy an entire village. He had seen it too many times, but he couldn't share that horror with Caroline.

"Has the St. Louis Police Department been called?" Thad asked the head security guard. He was in his fifties with a buzz cut and ex-military demeanor. Despite the fact that the boy might have just wandered off, the man had still sent his guards off with urgency to look everywhere for Mark. "My brother is Detective Ash Kendall—"

"You're Thad Kendall, the reporter," the head guard, Ron Thurston, interrupted. "I've seen you on the news." He probably wasn't talking about Thad's special reports on ZNN but rather the local reports about the shooting and the Christmas Eve Murders.

"Do you think the police need to be called?" Caroline asked, her face turning stark white as horror widened her tear-reddened eyes. "Do you think someone has kidnapped him?"

"We need to find him as soon as possible," Thad explained.

She blinked as if to dry her eyes and stared hard at him. "You didn't answer my question."

"I can't," he admitted, frustration eating at him. "I don't know."

"It's a possibility," the guard remarked, "given who you are."

"Has the entire building been searched?" Thad asked.

He needed to do it himself. He couldn't trust these guards to have conducted a thorough search. The ones under Ron were just kids, probably high-schoolers with no guns or badges or any real authority. He couldn't even trust his brother.

He reached for Ron's shoulder to guide him away from Caroline so that he wouldn't mention anything else about ransom within her hearing. "Show me where the public can't access—"

Caroline clutched his arm, holding him back from heading off with the guard. "Where are you going?"

"I'm going to look for him," he said. "You stay here, where you were supposed to meet me." By the carousel, where he would have found them had he showed up when they'd planned.

Caroline nodded. "I'll wait for him…and *you*…here." Before she released him, she squeezed his arm hard. "Find our son."

"I will," he promised.

Leaving her wrenched his heart. She turned toward the carousel, and her shoulders shook with sobs. He had managed no more than a few steps away from her when he heard a voice call out.

"Mommy, don't cry.…"

He turned back in time to see Caroline drop to her knees and throw her arms around their son. When he hurried over to them, Mark glanced up from his mother's shoulder. "You're here now, Daddy."

It was the first time his son had called him…anything to his face. Like Caroline, Thad felt like crying, too.

"Where were you?" Thad asked. "Were you looking for me?"

Had he caused this whole nightmare?

Mark shook his head. "I was waiting to see Santa but someone grabbed my hand."

Alarm kicked Thad's heart rate into overdrive. "Who grabbed you?"

Mark shrugged his thin shoulders. "I dunno. I didn't really see him. He was very tall, and the mall was so crowded that people were jammed in all around us."

And the boy was too short to see much above anyone's waist.

"But you know it was a man?"

"His hand was big," Mark replied, "like yours."

Thad settled his hand, which was shaking, onto the little boy's head. "Did he hurt you?"

Caroline gasped as she realized what Thad was really asking their son. She pulled back from the little boy and studied his face. "Are you all right?"

"I'm good."

"Is he okay?" the head security guard asked, concern in his voice.

With a glance, Thad deferred to Caroline. She knew their son best.

She nodded.

"So we can open the doors?" the guard asked Thad, deferring to him.

He hesitated because he wanted to pull every man into a lineup for his son to pick out his almost-abductor. "You really didn't see his face?" he asked the boy.

"No. He was wearing those kind of light-colored pants." He glanced at Thad's khakis. "Like yours." And probably half the other guys in the mall.

The guard must have come to the same conclusion because he said, "He's okay. Probably someone just accidently grabbed the wrong kid. This place is a zoo tonight, and if we don't open those doors soon, we may have a riot."

Thad sighed. He had no right to hold the entire mall hostage, and if he wasn't a Kendall, the guard would probably have not even agreed to the lockdown in the first place.

"Yeah, go ahead." He reached out his hand and shook Ron's. "And thank you for your fast response."

"I have five grandkids," the guard said with a grin. "I would have been going crazy, too, if one of them went missing." He headed off, his radio at his mouth.

Despite the crowded mall, the three of them

were suddenly very alone and very quiet as all the nerves gave way to relief and shock.

Mark glanced from his mother's face to Thad's, and then his bottom lip began to tremble as he realized the extent of their concern. "Am I in trouble?"

"No," Thad assured his son. "You didn't do anything wrong."

"You weren't supposed to leave the line," Caroline corrected them both. "Why did you let the man pull you away?"

The little boy's face flushed with bright color. "I thought the man was—" he turned back to Thad "—you."

"I wouldn't take you anywhere without telling your mother first," he said.

"I pulled away," Mark said, "when I saw it wasn't you."

"You saw his face?" He glanced in the direction in which the guard had walked off, thinking about calling him back to keep the doors locked.

"No," Mark said. "But he was wearing gloves." He touched Thad's bare and cold-chapped hands. "And you always forget to wear your gloves."

A giggle slipped from Caroline's lips at the boy's precocious observation.

"How did you get away from him?" Thad asked, his guts too tense to find any amusement in the situation. He wasn't as convinced as the guard that someone had just grabbed the wrong kid.

Mark shrugged. "I pulled loose. But it's so crowded I couldn't see anything. I couldn't find you, Mommy." His breath hitched, and his lip trembled more. "I kept looking, but it was so busy."

Caroline wrapped her arms tight around the little boy. "You found me. You're safe now," she assured him and herself.

"How did you find us?" Thad asked, wondering if the man who'd grabbed him had led him back to the carousel. Then it might have been just an honest mistake.

"I heard the merry-go-round and kept coming to where it got louder."

Damn. Now Thad was going to have to start liking Christmas music again. It had led their son back to them.

His hand shaking harder, he barely managed to gently pat the boy's head. "You're so smart."

Mark blinked up at him, as if the compliment alone had brought him to tears. He flashed back to his father complimenting him once, on a story he'd written in elementary school. Because his father was always so busy and distracted with business, the fact that he'd read the paper had been compliment enough, but then he'd told Thad that he'd done a good job. Effusive praise it wasn't, but Thad had been moved to tears, too.

He vowed then that he would be a better father. He would praise his son so much that a compliment wouldn't overwhelm the boy. And he would never again disappoint him as he almost had tonight. If the man who'd grabbed him had really intended to kidnap him, Thad might have lost him.

And if he lost Mark, he would lose Caroline, too. She loved their son so much. Like she had, Thad dropped to his knees and wrapped his arms around them both—holding them close to his madly pounding heart.

THE LITTLE BOY SLEPT peacefully, his lips curved into a sweet smile as if he dreamed only happy dreams. Caroline wouldn't sleep at all tonight. She wouldn't dare to even close her eyes for fear of reliving those nightmarish moments when Mark had been missing. Images of what could have happened kept flitting through her mind even with her eyes wide-open, though.

As she turned down the brightness of the lamp next to his bed, she studied the picture propped up against the fire-engine base of the lamp. That was what had brought the smile to her little boy's face.

His dream.

The picture wasn't just of him sitting on Santa's lap but of Caroline and Thad kneeling next to him as he told the costumed mall worker what he wanted for Christmas. In order to make the night less traumatic for Mark, they'd let him talk to Santa. And the other people, knowing that the boy had gone missing for a while, had let them cut in line. So the little boy had gotten his picture with Santa—the picture he wanted to be a reality.

A family.

While tonight had had a happy ending, Mark's dream wouldn't. It would never be realized…at least not with Thad. After one lingering gaze at her son, she left the room and headed down the stairs to where Thad waited in the living room.

He had shut off the lamps, so that the only light came from the fire flickering in the hearth. But he hadn't dimmed the lights to seduce her. He didn't even turn toward her. His entire focus was on the street outside the window in front of which he stood.

"You don't believe it was an accident tonight," she said, "that some dad or grandpa grabbed the wrong kid in the crowd."

"I have no reason to think that isn't exactly what happened," he replied, and he finally turned away from the window.

She walked up to it now, but she could only see her own reflection in the glass. Dark circles rimmed her eyes; they were the only color in her pale face.

"What does that mean?" she wondered. "That you don't see anyone out there? That no one's made any threats?"

He nodded. "Both."

"But you're a Kendall," she said, remembering the security guard's awe at the realization. "And that puts anyone close to you in danger."

He tensed. "How's that?"

"Your family has a lot of money," Caroline said, as if he needed the reminder. Maybe he did. He had been gone a long time, maybe long enough to forget that the Kendalls were St. Louis royalty. "Someone could think that kidnapping your son for ransom is a way to get some of that money."

He chuckled. "My family has a lot of money. I don't." Then his brow furrowed. "I have stock, though. And with what Uncle Craig and Devin have done with the company over the years…"

"You're worth a lot of money," she said. That had never mattered to him, though, and it had certainly never mattered to her. Their relationship might have stood a better chance at surviving had he had no money.

"But no one even knows I have a son," he said.

Caroline sucked in a breath at the pain that jabbed her over his offhand admission. He had told no one about Mark? Was he ashamed of his son or of his son's mother?

"There's just so much going on right now," he said. "There's something else I have to tell my sister." He uttered a ragged sigh. "And it's such a media circus around the estate. I don't want to bring you and Mark into that craziness."

She nodded as if she understood. But she really had no idea what he was going through. She had no clue what it was like to be one of the infamous Kendalls who had grown up under the shadow of such tragedy.

"It doesn't matter that you haven't told anybody," she said, even though it did matter. To her. "All anyone would have to do is see the two of you together to know that Mark is your son."

He pushed his hand through his hair almost as if he was grabbing at the strands. "That's why the mall was such a bad idea for so many reasons."

"You don't want anyone knowing you have a son," she realized. It wasn't just for all the reasons he'd mentioned, either. There were reasons he hadn't mentioned, secrets he was keeping.

"Caroline—"

"Who are you?" she asked. "Really?"

He threw her words back at her. "You're the one who said my being a Kendall puts him at risk."

"But that's not why you've put him at risk," she said. "It's because of whatever you really are." She'd always sensed there was so much more to Thad Kendall, that there was a darkness and ruthlessness that came from more than reporting stories.

"You keep saying that…and it makes no

sense." He shrugged as if brushing off her concerns. "You know who I am."

She shook her head. "No. Even when we were together, I knew you were holding back from me, that there was more to you than anyone else knew."

"I never held back with *you*," he said, his voice low and husky. He moved close behind her so that his chest pressed tight against her back.

Her skin tingled as his breath teased her neck before his lips touched it. "I wouldn't be holding back now if you weren't making me."

"Nobody stops Thad Kendall from doing what he wants," she remarked bitterly, reminding herself that he'd had no problem leaving her last time.

But he must have taken her words as a challenge or an invitation because he turned her toward him and closed his arms around her. Now they were pressed chest to breasts. His chest was hard and muscular, and her breasts were full and sensitive and rising and falling with her now labored breathing.

He groaned, and his eyes dilated, the pupils swallowing the sapphire-blue. The attraction between them was even stronger than it had been four years ago.

Passion zipped through her veins, but she couldn't give in to it. She couldn't give in to him. "Thad…"

He took her open lips as an invitation, too, settling his mouth firmly onto hers. His lips moved over hers, and then his tongue slid between, tangling with hers, teasing her.

A moan tore from her throat as need coursed through her. She had never desired any man the way she wanted Thad. But wanting Thad was pointless when she would never be able to keep him. She wriggled free of his arms.

"I don't want you," she said.

"Do you really want me to prove you're lying again?" he challenged as he made a move to pull her back into his arms.

She stumbled back, out of his reach. "I don't want you unless I can have *all* of you," she said. "Unless you'll tell me the secrets that I know you're keeping from me and probably from everyone else who cares about you."

"Caroline, you don't know what you're talking—"

"I know that you're not just a photojournalist," she said, trusting her instincts. As a single mother, she had learned to trust them. Tonight they'd failed her because she never should have taken that call. "And I just hope like hell that whatever you really are hasn't put our son in danger."

ED TOUCHED THE COPY he had bought of the boy's picture with Santa. It sat on the passenger's seat beside him. He had his answer now…about what mattered most to Thad Kendall. After days of following the guy, which hadn't been easy since Kendall was an expert defensive driver, he'd figured out what no one else had about the infamous photojournalist.

The nomadic bachelor had a family. But he wouldn't have them for much longer.

His hand shaking, Ed touched the boy's face. "I almost had you tonight."

First he had distracted the woman with the call. Because she was one of those teachers who always wanted to be available to her students and their parents, it had been easy enough to get her cell number off the website of the elementary school where she taught and to which Ed had followed her one morning. It had even been easy to grab the boy's hand and lead him away from the line.

But when the kid had pulled free, Ed hadn't pursued him. There had been too many people around, which at first he'd thought would work in his favor so no one would notice him. But there had also been security guards around, and Kendall had had the foresight to order the exits locked down.

Ed wouldn't have escaped with the boy. So he had let him go.

Then he had watched them all play happy family with Santa. Now, after personally witnessing how much the kid meant to Kendall, Ed was more determined than ever.

Lights of a passing car shone through his windshield, so he hunched down in his seat. He wasn't parked where Kendall could see him, but this was the kind of neighborhood where strange cars were noticed and reported.

He couldn't be discovered yet. All these years had passed, and everyone who'd mattered to Ed had passed. But it wouldn't be over until everyone who mattered to Thad Kendall was gone, too.

He reached across the leather console and skimmed his finger over the boy's picture. "Next time you won't get away."

Chapter Six

Thad hadn't slept at all the night before and not just because he'd spent the night sitting in his car keeping watch over Caroline's house but because her words had haunted him.

"And I just hope like hell that whatever you really are hasn't put our son in danger."

He needed to know if she was right to be concerned. He glanced around the St. Louis Police Department's interrogation room, hoping the cement block walls and thick mirror made this a secure place for the call he'd had to place.

"Are you sure my cover hasn't been blown?" he asked his boss.

"There's been no chatter about it," Anya said. "But they could have a code word for you, something we haven't cracked yet."

"Crack it!" he snapped, his nerves frayed

from lack of sleep and the horror of those long moments his son had been missing.

"It's not that easy, and you know it," she replied with strained patience.

"Yeah, I know...."

"Has something happened?" she asked. "Has there been an attempt on your life?"

"No." But if Mark had been abducted, there would have been. If the fear of losing the boy hadn't killed Thad, Caroline would have managed the deed with her bare hands. And he wouldn't have blamed her.

"But you have cause for concern?" she asked, ever the professional. The woman never lost her cool.

Usually, neither did Thad. "I have concern."

"I know why you went home," she reminded him. "Your parents' murderer is still out there. Is that the reason for your concern?"

"It's the reason I needed out of my last assignment," he said. "But if my leaving got Michaels killed…"

"You couldn't have saved him."

"We'll never know for sure," he stubbornly maintained just as he had when she'd tried to absolve him of his guilt during their last conversation.

"I'll let you know when we break the code," she said, and then clicked off.

Thad sighed as he pocketed his phone.

"What will you never know for sure?" Ash asked from the open door to the interrogation room.

Lack of sleep must have dulled his reflexes, because he hadn't even heard the door open. He shrugged but answered honestly, "Work stuff."

"Isn't knowing for sure part of your job?" Ash asked. "All that digging until you get to the truth? You're kind of famous for it."

Thad narrowed his eyes in suspicion. "You're complimenting me?" Like their father, it wasn't something his older brothers had ever really done. They'd been more likely to beat the crap out of him and each other.

They had only ever been careful with Natalie because she'd always seemed so fragile. As adults, and after what she'd been through, they all knew better now. She wasn't easily broken. But still Thad stalled over telling her the truth of her paternity, wanting to protect her as he and his brothers always had.

Ash shrugged his massive shoulders. "Just

stating a fact. You're good at getting to the truth."

Not so much at telling it, though. "It's my job."

"I'm glad you're back," Ash admitted. "We've all been working on this, but we need fresh eyes. We need *your* eyes." He glanced at the boxes of tapes Thad had set on the table next to the bracket where a suspect's hand-cuffs were clipped. "What's all this? Did you find another lead?"

"I don't know," he admitted. He would hate to think that last night had anything to do with his parents' murders. Or worse, with his dual career, as Caroline had accused. "But I need to have someone look at a few hours of this security footage. We need to find out who might have grabbed a three-year-old kid last night at the mall."

"There was no report of a kidnapping!" Ash exclaimed with all the horror of a man about to become a father himself. Then he nodded in sudden realization. "But I did hear about some kind of security issue at the mall. The exit doors were momentarily locked down, so no one could leave until the situation had been resolved."

"The kid got away from whoever grabbed

him. He's not hurt." He hadn't even been all that shaken up until he'd noticed how scared his mother and father had been. Mark was one tough little guy. He was definitely a Kendall. Pride warmed Thad's heart along with the love that swelled it whenever he thought of his son.

"What happened?" Ash asked. "And how the hell do you know about it? I didn't think you were working for your network here. I thought you were just going to focus on family right now."

For once.

Ash didn't say it, but Thad heard the unsaid accusation that clearly glittered with a brief flash of resentment in his green eyes. Ash had left home for a while, for the service, but he'd come right back to St. Louis after his term was up. He hadn't kept going back overseas like Thad.

"I was focusing on family," Thad insisted.

"At the mall?" Ash scoffed. "You hate the mall. I saw your face when Gray was kidding about Christmas shopping a few days ago. You've never gotten over your aversion to Christmas. So what the hell were you doing at the mall *this* time of year?"

Thad drew in a deep breath and then admitted, "Going with my son to see Santa."

"Son?" Ash's voice rose with shock. "You have a son?"

He nodded. "His name is Mark. He's three years old."

"And you're just telling me about him now?" Hurt dimmed the anger in Ash's eyes. "Does anyone else know you have a son?"

"Until a few days ago, I didn't know myself," he said.

"But he's three years old...." Ash nodded as if he'd done some math in his head. "And you've been gone longer than that. Are you sure he's yours?"

Thad hadn't asked to use the interrogation room just to make his call in privacy. He clicked the remote and turned on the TV in the corner. The security footage in the DVD was paused on his son's face. "You tell me what you think."

"Damn." Ash grinned. "He's you all over again. Cute little shit."

"Smart, too," Thad said.

Ash whistled. "Wow. You're already talking like a proud papa. Who's the mama? I don't even remember you dating anyone when you were home last. But you weren't around much. You were working on some special assignment at the local station."

"Her name is Caroline Emerson," he said. "She's an elementary school teacher."

Ash laughed. "Okay. I get why you didn't mention her."

"Why?" he asked. Caroline might have thought him a snob for not introducing her, but his own brother should know him better.

"Aunt Angela would've been planning your wedding if she'd met her."

His brother did know him better, and they both knew their aunt too well. "Yeah, she would have been ordering flowers and booking St. Luke's."

"Sounds like she should have been," Ash pointed out. "So you didn't know she was pregnant when you left?"

"She didn't even know yet," he said. Had Caroline known, she would have told him. He believed that she would have tried to contact him, too, had she not feared his family would think her a gold digger. She should have tried to get word to him after their son had been born, but he couldn't blame her if she'd wanted to protect the little boy from the fishbowl life of a Kendall.

"Would it have made a difference?" Ash

wondered, staring at the boy on the TV.
"Would you have stayed home?"

Remembering the importance of the mission he'd left to carry out, he shook his head.
But he would have returned as soon as he'd
been able to make sure both Caroline and
Mark were okay.

"What about now?" his older brother
asked. "Will you leave now?"

Subject to an intensity that had him
squirming and unable to lie, Thad suddenly
had insight into how Detective Kendall conducted an interrogation. "Once our parents'
killer is caught I will go back to my job."

"Why does your job have to be over there?"
Ash wondered. "Why can't it be here?"

"Local news has no interest for me," he
said. Because it had nothing to do with his
real job.

"What about your son and his mother?
What's your interest in them?" The detective continued his interrogation.

"Right now I just want to make sure they're
safe," Thad said, getting irritated with his
brother and probably with his own inability
to answer Ash's questions.

"So protectiveness only?" Ash persisted.

"Stop interrogating me," Thad snapped. "I

need to know if someone tried to grab my son. And if so, I need your help to protect him and his mother!"

Ash squeezed his shoulder with reassurance. "He's my nephew. I'll help you look out for him. He's a Kendall."

Actually, he wasn't. Caroline had given the boy her last name. But Thad wanted Emerson changed to Kendall, as soon as he knew for certain that he wasn't putting them in danger.

CAROLINE'S HAND SHOOK as she held the telephone. It was the cordless house phone. Thad had taken her cell the night before, so that his detective brother could try to track down the person who had called her while she and Mark had been at the mall.

"Thank you for taking Mark tonight," she told Tammy. "I was freaking him out with being so nervous and overprotective." She hadn't dared to leave the house despite Saturday being their usual errand day. She hadn't gone anywhere, and she hadn't even let Mark play in the yard. "Is he okay?"

"Yes," her best friend assured her, "he and Steven Jr. and Steven Sr. are playing video games and having a great time."

Steven Jr. was three years older than Mark,

and until her son had met his own father, he'd idolized the older boy and his dad. Now he had his own daddy. And he had asked about him the moment he'd awakened.

"Of course, you're probably freaking out even more that you're not here to watch over him yourself," Tammy commiserated. "You must have been so scared last night."

"Yes." But not just last night; she couldn't shake off her fear. "I just wish I knew if he's really safe, though." She hadn't been able to sleep last night; she'd sat beside his bed, watching over him.

"We're staying home with the burglar alarm on. Steve and I won't let anything happen to him," Tammy assured her.

"I know." Caroline expelled a shuddery breath of relief. "I trust you." More than she trusted her own ability to keep him safe given how she had nearly lost him the night before.

"What about Thad?" Tammy asked. "Do you trust him?"

"Not as far as I can throw him." She couldn't trust him when she was convinced that he wasn't being honest with her.

"But he stepped up last night," her romantic friend reminded her. "He was there for you."

And he was here now, pulling his car into her driveway.

"Tammy, there's no chance of anything more between me and Thad," she cautioned her friend and her own foolish heart, which sped up its beat as soon as he stepped from his car.

All long legs and lean hips in slim-fitting jeans, he was so damn sexy. The wind played with his dark hair, tousling it and sprinkling it with snowflakes. He lifted a gloveless hand, as Mark had noticed, and pushed his hair back from his forehead. Then moments later he was ringing her doorbell; it echoed throughout the living room.

"Who's there?" Tammy asked.

"I have to go…."

"Don't open that door," Tammy advised her, "until you make sure it's safe."

She and Thad alone in the house damn well weren't safe, but she wanted to hear whatever he'd learned today. "It's okay."

"It's Thad," Tammy said with a triumphant giggle. "Have fun!"

Shaking her head at her friend's hopeless romanticism, Caroline opened the door.

"Did I do something wrong already?" he

asked, noting her head shake. "Or is that still?"

"You tell me." Despite the warning bells ringing inside her head, Caroline stepped back to let him inside and closed the door behind him.

"Where's the little man?"

"At my friend Tammy's."

He tensed. "Is that a good idea?"

"Given how well I watched him at the mall, it's a great idea," she said, berating herself. "Tammy's never lost one of her children."

In addition to Steven Jr., she had a three-year-old daughter, Bethany. The little girl adored Mark, but he only tolerated her. Now. Tammy swore that someday they would get married.

Thad cupped her shoulders and squeezed them. "Stop beating yourself up about last night," he admonished. "You didn't do anything wrong."

"I never should have taken that call."

"You wouldn't have if I'd showed up when I was supposed to," he said, shouldering the blame himself. "And you really just glanced down for a second. I saw it on the security tape."

Fear quickened her pulse. "Did you see who grabbed him?"

He shook his head. "It was such a crowd. We couldn't even find Mark on any of the security footage except by the carousel."

"We?"

"My brother helped me go through the tapes." He sighed. "He knows about you and Mark, which means—" he glanced at his wrist watch "—that by now my whole family probably knows."

"Shouldn't you have told them yourself?" she asked, hurt that he wouldn't have chosen to make such an announcement personally.

"I would have," he said. "But I'm sure Ash didn't trust me to do it, so he spilled."

"You should go to them," she urged, worried about his family's reaction. The Kendalls weren't the type to have children out of wedlock. If Thad hadn't introduced her before because he'd thought his family wouldn't consider her worthy of a Kendall, they would probably hate her now. "Explain that you didn't know, that I didn't tell you…"

"You seem in an awful hurry to get rid of me." His blue eyes narrowed. "Are you worried about being alone with me?"

She forced a yawn despite the adrenaline coursing through her at his nearness. His hands still cupped her shoulders, kneading her flesh. "I didn't sleep last night. I was going to head up to bed soon."

"Don't let me stop you." He caught her hand and tugged her toward the stairs.

"Thad, this is a bad idea." But even she heard how halfhearted her protest was. And she followed him up the stairs to the room he must have instinctively known was hers.

"I just want to hold you," he said, and now he tugged her toward the queen sleigh bed that was still neatly made because she hadn't even slept in it. "I'm tired, too. I couldn't sleep last night and then I spent hours going over that mall footage today, trying to convince myself that our son is safe."

"He's safe tonight," she assured him. She was the one in danger now, of falling for the man who'd already broken her heart.

While he had had no warning and no training, he was proving to be a good dad, patient and loving. And with her, he was attentive and reassuring and protective.

And so damn sexy.

She was tired, though, too tired to fight feelings for him that had never gone away even when he had.

"Let me make sure you're safe," he said. "Let me stay with you."

She shook her head. "Your staying puts me in more danger than your leaving."

"I'll just hold you," Thad said.

Was that really all he wanted? Because she wanted—she *needed*—more.

He let go of her hands to pull back the comforter and the soft flannel sheets. "I just want to hold you in my arms tonight."

And that was the problem. Caroline wanted to spend every night in his arms. But Thad would never give her forever.

Whatever he really was—and it wasn't just a reporter—had a tighter hold on his heart than she and their son ever would. But if whatever he was put Mark in danger, then his heart would get broken, too. He would never forgive himself for causing their son harm.

And neither would Caroline....

Chapter Seven

Just as he'd promised, Thad had held Caroline in his arms all night. She had slept peacefully. But, like the night before, he had been unable to close his eyes. He hadn't wanted to take his gaze from her beautiful face. And his body had been too tense and achy with desire for him to relax enough to sleep.

He could have seduced her with kisses and caresses. Even though four years had passed, he remembered in vivid detail exactly what drove her crazy. A kiss on the back of her neck. A caress on the side of her breast, his thumb teasing ever closer toward the tight nipple.

And because he had been so tempted to seduce her, he hadn't. He didn't want to coerce her into making love with him. She would regret it and resent him.

He had already given her reason enough

to resent him. So he'd forced himself to leave her first thing in the morning, before she awakened, before he gave in to temptation. But as he pulled into the nearly full driveway at the Kendall estate, he wished he'd stayed with Caroline instead.

With a groan he shut off his car, stepped out and headed into the three-story mansion. Someone must have been watching for his car because they all met him in the entryway, as if they were throwing him a surprise party. He wasn't particularly surprised, though. Over the years he had developed the intuition to detect an ambush.

"Thanks a lot," he told Ash, who grinned unrepentantly.

Natalie smacked Thad's shoulder. "I can't believe you didn't tell us you have a son."

"Someone didn't give me the chance." He glared at his older brother.

"You're not really great about using your chances to disclose information," Gray remarked with a sideways glance at his fiancée.

Thad needed to talk to Natalie—she deserved to know the truth about her parentage. But he understood it would hurt her, and she'd already been hurt enough.

"Well, I've been a little busy finding out

that I'm a father," he said in an effort to excuse himself.

"Are you sure?" Uncle Craig asked as he led the group back to the family room with its cathedral ceiling and French doors that opened onto the brick patio. Sometime over the past four years, or maybe just the past four months since it was revealed that his brother's killer was still out there, Craig Kendall had aged. His hair was completely silver now. "Did you have a DNA test done yet?"

Thad reached for his wallet and the picture Caroline had given him after Mark's brief disappearance. But before he could pull it out, Ash produced a printout of the surveillance photo.

Probably dressed for church, in a brightly patterned, stylish suit, Aunt Angela hurried after him, her heels clicking against the wood floor. She grabbed for the grainy picture but then took Thad's proffered colored snapshot, too. "Oh, my…"

Tears glittered in her warm brown eyes as she focused on Mark's little face. Thad grinned at her emotional reaction. "So, what do you think, Auntie, do I need a DNA test?"

Aunt Angela lifted her gaze from the pictures to Thad. "He looks just like you when you were that age." She smiled. "Now I know why you took the old photo albums out of the library."

Natalie leaned over their petite aunt's shoulder to see the pictures. "Oh, he's *so* cute. I don't remember Thad ever being that cute."

"Hey!" he protested.

"What's his name?" Rachel asked as Aunt Angela passed the pictures to her. She sat in the chair Ash had helped her into given her swollen belly.

"Mark."

"His mother must be beautiful," Natalie said, "for him to be so cute."

"She is," Thad said. So beautiful that he ached for her.

Devin wound his arm around Jolie's waist. "You'll make beautiful babies then, my love."

Aunt Angela patted Rachel's belly. "Our family is growing," she said with a mother's pride. And, truth be told, she'd been much more maternal to them than their biological mother had ever been.

"When do we get to meet your son?" Uncle Craig asked. His blue eyes held some skepticism yet. Despite how much Mark looked like him, his uncle wasn't entirely convinced of his paternity.

"He's at St. Luke's church right now with his mother." That was the church that Aunt Angela had occasionally convinced them all to attend.

"You should have gone along," Ash teased him. "You could use some saving."

If he only knew.…

There was no saving him from what he had to do now. "Hey, Nat, I need a few minutes alone with you."

Her forehead creased, but she nodded her agreement.

As they left the family room, he overheard Devin asking Aunt Angela to add the owner of Turner Connections to the Christmas guest list. But their generous aunt, who lived by the motto of the more the merrier, declined, "It should be just family."

"This'll be his first Christmas without his wife," Devin pointed out.

"You're not doing business on the holidays," she scolded. "Family only."

Would Natalie feel as if she was still family once he revealed her true paternity?

She followed him up the stairs that led to the wing with their bedrooms. He had his own suite for his use whenever he was in town, which hadn't been often over the past several years.

"I was in your room last time because you were crying out," she mused. "Why do I think I'm going to be the one crying now?"

Because she was damn smart; she always had been.

"This isn't easy to tell you...."

"And everyone else already knows," she surmised. "They've all been calling and checking on me, waiting for you to break whatever news you must have decided you needed to be the one to break to me." She chuckled at her own joke. "But I guess that's kind of your area though, *breaking news*."

He just hoped it wouldn't break her, but then he reminded himself she wasn't that fragile little girl anymore who'd discovered their parents' dead bodies. "This isn't going to change anything."

She groaned. "God, this is bad."

"Nat—"

"When someone says this isn't going to change anything, you know it's going to change *everything*." She grabbed his hands and held on tight. "Just tell me, Thad. I can handle it."

All her life, he and his brothers had tried

to protect her because they'd never forgiven themselves that she'd been the one to find their murdered parents. But when he'd come back just in time to shoot her stalker, he'd finally realized that his little sister had grown into one tough young woman.

He dragged in a breath of air and then told her, "That guy I shot—"

"You found out who he was?" she asked hopefully.

He shook his head. "Well, we don't know his name."

"I thought it was Wade…something…"

"We don't know his last name yet." Or if his first name was even really Wade.

"But you do know something about him," she surmised. *Damn smart…*

He nodded. "He's your brother."

She laughed. "Yeah, right. Like I don't have enough big brothers…"

"He's your half brother, Natalie. Something about him looked familiar to me—"

"You thought he looked like me!" She shuddered.

He squeezed her hands back as she held his yet. "So I had his DNA run. They put it against what we had of yours from the hospital. And Ash and Devin and I gave samples of ours."

She gulped in a breath, as if fighting down hysteria. But her voice was steady when she said, "So he's just my brother. Not yours or Ash or Devin's."

"Yes."

She nodded. Despite how tough she was acting, tears began to streak down her face as she put it all together. "So Daddy wasn't really my dad."

"I'm sorry," he said. "So sorry...and if I'd known he was your brother..."

"You still would have had to kill him," she said, "or he would have killed me and Gray. You did the right thing."

"If there's anything I can do..."

The door creaked open behind him, as if someone had been listening outside it. Gray walked in and crossed the room to his fiancée, pulling her into his arms. "I've got this," he assured Thad.

She clung to him as if using his strength to shore up her own. As separate people they were strong, as a couple they were invincible. Thad, who had vowed to always remain single, envied the strength of their union.

As he backed toward the door to give them

privacy, Natalie lifted her head from Gray's shoulder. "You can do something for me," she told him.

"Anything, Nat."

"Find out who my father was." From the grim look on her beautiful face, she wasn't looking for a tearful reunion.

Like Thad, she was looking for a killer.

CAROLINE SLIPPED INTO the back row of church. She was late. She must not have set her alarm before she'd fallen asleep in Thad's arms. Wanting him as she did, she didn't know how she'd managed to sleep. Just sleep.

Thad Kendall had kept his word. He had only held her, his strong arms wrapped tight around her the entire night. She'd enforced her no-sex rule so that she wouldn't fall for him again. But because he'd abided by that rule when they both knew he could have seduced her at any time, she was in even more danger of falling for him than if they'd made love all night.

God, she was such a fool. She and Mark attended church every Sunday, and usually she prayed for peace and food for starving children. Today she intended to pray for wisdom.

She needed it to remind her of all the reasons she shouldn't be in love with Thad Kendall.

But then her son wriggled out from between Tammy and Steve Stehouwer and ran down the aisle toward her. And she remembered the most important reason she loved Thad—he had given her their son. No matter how much he'd hurt her when he'd left last time and how much he would hurt her when he left again, he had given her the greatest treasure of her life.

"Mommy!" Mark squealed as he squeezed into the row next to her.

Caroline lifted him in her arms and hugged him close. "Shh…"

But instead of looking at them with disapproval, the people around them were chuckling or smiling. Her son always won the heart of everyone with whom he came in contact; he was that sweet and lovable.

She pressed a kiss to his forehead and then his cheek and then his chin. He giggled and wriggled down to stand beside her.

His hand slid into hers. "I missed you, Mommy."

"I missed you, too." The words brought back those horrible moments that he'd disappeared at the mall. What if he'd been gone longer? Or worse yet, what if he'd never been found?

Panic clutched her heart in a tight grip. And she forgot all about praying for wisdom. She prayed for her son to stay safe. As she prayed, goose bumps lifted on her skin. Someone had opened the door and let in a blast of winter air.

But the cold wasn't what caused the goose bumps; it was that eerie sense of foreboding that had chills chasing up and down her spine.

She'd had the same sensation at the mall. Like she had then, she looked around for someone watching her. Several people were still smiling at Mark and her. She smiled back despite the tension gnawing at her. But she kept looking around until she encountered an unsmiling face.

The older man's mouth was drawn tight, almost into a frown of disapproval, as he stared at her. She didn't know his name, but with his silver hair and intense gaze, he looked familiar to her.

Had she seen him in church before? Or had she seen him that night at the mall?

She leaned down to whisper to Mark. "Honey, do you remember—"

"Shh, Mommy, you gotta be quiet in church," he remembered. *Now*.

"But this is important, honey," she continued. "I need to know if you—"

But when she looked up, the man was gone. Had he taken off because she'd seen him and he was worried that Mark might have identified him as the man who'd grabbed him at the mall?

And if he was the same man, then Mark had not been grabbed by accident.

Someone was after her son.

MAYBE ED SHOULD HAVE taken down the dated wallpaper in the kitchen, but Emily had put it up when they'd gotten married. This was the first house they had ever lived in as man and wife. They hadn't lived there long, but sweet, sentimental Emily had never let him sell the house when they'd moved into a bigger and nicer one.

He had rented out the little bungalow over the years with the stipulation that no one touch the wallpaper.

The last person who'd lived there had respected that, but he was gone now. So Ed was using the house again. And he had finally papered over Emily's teapot wallpaper—with pictures of Thad Kendall.

The man was young, only thirty-one, but he had been all over the world—more than once. There were photos of him in every country as long as it was the scene of civil unrest or all-out war.

The photojournalist thrived on danger. He'd come out of some of the most dangerous places in the world alive. So killing him wouldn't have been easy. Or even all that satisfying....

There were recent photos of him, too, cut from local newspapers. Every day they ran a story about Thad Kendall being forced to kill to save his sister.

Forced to kill?

Ed doubted that it had been a hardship for the man. And he certainly didn't appear, in any of the photos, to be struggling with guilt or regret. A true killer, he wasn't suffering over what he'd done.

Not like Ed had suffered. Not like he was suffering now, shaking with the need for a drink. But he couldn't dull his pain with alcohol because it also dulled his wits. And he needed his wits about him to deal with Thad Kendall.

Thad needed to suffer, and Ed needed to make certain that he did. It was only too bad that to make Kendall suffer, the woman and the boy would have to suffer, too.

Ed had added pictures of them to his collection of Thad. The woman working at school and shopping at the store and attending church. The boy playing at day care and shopping with his mom at the store, her hand always on his, and her holding him in church. And in the center of the collage was their picture with Santa, their family photo.

But like Ed's, their family would not be together much longer.

Chapter Eight

NERVES TIGHTENED THAD'S stomach, and he felt like a kid again, caught doing something wrong and waiting for his punishment. Since the age of eleven, Thad had received his hugs, encouragement and affection from Aunt Angela. Those were things he'd rarely had when his parents had been alive.

And he'd received his punishment from Uncle Craig. Having to go to his office at Kendall Communications was tantamount to being sent to the principal's office. But he had never had any doubt that his uncle cared, that he loved him, and that was why he punished—to make him a better man.

Thad wished that he could be the kind of father to Mark that Uncle Craig had been to him. But how was he going to do that from half a world away? Unlike Thad's father, Uncle Craig had always put raising the kids before the business, and it hadn't suffered any.

But running a communication company and doing what Thad did when he was *reporting* a story were two entirely different things. Uncle Craig had never put them in any danger because of what he did. But when the man arrested for their parents' murders had been cleared, Thad had wondered if their father had done something that had motivated the killings. He had been ruthless about getting ahead in business, just as ruthless as Thad was when getting the information he needed.

The door creaked open, startling Thad into whirling toward the entrance. Uncle Craig chuckled at his uneasiness. "Take you back?"

"Getting called to your office?" Thad sighed. "Oh, yeah…"

"You didn't have to come here as often as your brothers did," Uncle Craig said.

Thad grinned. "That's because I was the better brother."

Uncle Craig laughed harder. "You were probably the worst. You were just better at not getting caught."

The truth of his former guardian's statement elicited a laugh from Thad, too. That ability of which Uncle Craig spoke had gotten him out of trouble in his youth and had saved his life over the past several years.

"You got caught this time, though," Uncle Craig mused.

Thad tensed. Had his uncle discovered the truth about him?

"When I disappeared yesterday morning, it was because I stopped by St. Luke's," Uncle Craig admitted.

"You saw Mark and Caroline?"

Uncle Craig nodded. "He is definitely your son."

Maybe that wasn't a good thing...for Mark. Maybe that was what had caused the incident at the mall, if in fact someone had tried to grab him. Even Ash wasn't sure since they hadn't been able to see anything sinister on the security footage.

Uncle Craig settled behind his mahogany desk and pulled out the middle drawer where he'd always kept his checkbook. Over the years Thad had come to this office for money more than he had for punishments. "How much does she want from you?" he asked.

"What?"

"For support. She's been raising this boy alone for three years," Uncle Craig reminded him. "She must want some compensation for all the expenses she covered on her own."

Thad shook his head. "Man, she was right...."

"About what?"

"The money," he replied.

Uncle Craig flipped open his checkbook as if getting ready to write down a figure.

Thad continued, "She said that was what you'd all think she wanted if she tried contacting any of you. It's why she didn't try to get a message to me when she realized she was pregnant."

Now he regretted getting angry with her when he'd discovered he had a son. Having not introduced her to his family when they'd dated, he'd left her in an untenable position.

Uncle Craig leaned back in his chair, his blue eyes narrowed in suspicion. "So she doesn't want money?"

They had never discussed it, which had Thad flinching with guilt. He'd grown up never having to think about a mortgage or a car loan or student loans, so he'd forgotten that most people didn't have that same luxury.

He should have offered her money. For the past three years she'd supported their son all by herself, and for the great job she'd done raising him, she deserved the whole Kendall fortune. But she had never asked for any money from him.

He shook his head in response to Uncle Craig's question.

"Then what does she want?"

Thad expelled a ragged sigh. "For me to not hurt Mark." Or her again.

Instead of defending or supporting him, Uncle Craig looked more worried than he had about the money. "Will you?"

Thinking of those horrible moments when the boy had disappeared, and of that white SUV Thad kept glimpsing in his rearview mirror, he shrugged. "I don't know."

"Being a father is a huge responsibility," the oldest Kendall said. "One I wish I'd taken more seriously when my son was little. I kept thinking we had all the time in the world."

His and Aunt Angela's only child had been just a few years older than Mark was now, six, when he died in a car accident.

"But we both know no one has as much

time as they think they have," Uncle Craig continued, "to spend with the people they love."

"What happened to Connor was a horrible, horrible accident," Thad said. One for which he suspected his aunt and uncle had blamed themselves for many years.

"As a parent, it's our responsibility to keep our children safe," Uncle Craig said, confirming Thad's suspicion and eliciting his own guilt.

If he had put Mark in danger…

"The boy's mother—"

"Caroline Emerson," Thad said, because she was so much more than just the mother of his child. He had loved her even before she'd given him a son.

"Caroline seemed especially nervous and protective, even in church," Uncle Craig remarked. "When she caught me watching them, she seemed truly frightened. I left quickly so I wouldn't upset her."

"Ash found out about Mark because of an incident at the mall. Didn't he tell you about it?" When he'd spilled Thad's secret…

Uncle Craig nodded his silver-haired head. "Yes. But he wasn't concerned about it. He wrote it off as the holiday crush and crowds at the mall."

Thad wished he could write it off as easily. But doubt and fear gnawed at him.

"But then Ash isn't a father quite yet," Uncle Craig continued, "so he doesn't have a parent's instincts. Caroline does, and she seems quite concerned about her son's safety."

"Our son," Thad automatically corrected him.

"What do your instincts say?" Uncle Craig asked.

Thad pushed a slightly shaking hand through his hair. "My instincts are overdeveloped," he admitted. "Because of the places I've been the past several years, I see danger everywhere."

"If you didn't, you wouldn't have survived," Uncle Craig said, his blue eyes bright with emotion. "And if you go back again, you may not."

He was used to his aunt begging him not to leave whenever he came home. But his uncle had always seemed to understand that it was something he needed to do.

"The first three years of that little boy's life, he didn't have a father," Uncle Craig reminded him. "Do you want him to grow up without one?"

"I just want him to grow up," Thad said, "safe and happy."

"So you do think he's in danger?"

Thad sighed. "I learned long ago that it doesn't matter where you are—a war-torn country or asleep in your own bed—you can be in danger."

"That's something you shouldn't have had to learn as young as you did," Uncle Craig said.

It was something Thad intended to do his damnedest to make sure Mark didn't learn for a long time.

WHEN SHE HAD AGREED to let Thad see Mark whenever he wanted, she hadn't considered how much he would want to. And how much that would make her want him.

He leaned over the bed and kissed Mark's forehead. "Good night, little buddy."

"Good night, Daddy," Mark murmured sleepily, his eyes already closed.

Caroline wished she could close her eyes and blot out the image of Thad Kendall as a loving father. It would have been better had he been unattached and uninvolved;

then Mark wouldn't miss him so much when he left.

And neither would she.

He joined her in the hall, pulling the door almost closed behind him. "I'll never get used to that."

"What?" she asked.

"Him calling me Daddy." He touched his chest, as if the word physically affected his heart.

Maybe it did. Caroline's heart was reacting, too. It beat faster at the sight of Thad in a black T-shirt that was molded to his muscular chest.

"Looks like you got wetter during his bath than he did," she remarked.

He chuckled. "Yeah, sorry about that. I'll clean up the bathroom."

She shook her head. "I already did when you were reading him his bedtime story."

A muscle twitched along his cheek. "A Christmas story…"

"Sorry," she said with a gentle smile. "Like most little kids, Mark loves Christmas." Because nothing bad had happened on any of his Christmases. Her heart ached for the pain Thad had suffered at such a young age.

"That's good," Thad said. "I'm glad. And

I'll make an effort to get over my aversion to it…for him."

"Finding your parents' killer would help you with that," she mused. "Are you any closer?"

He shook his head. "No. And that was the gift I really wanted to give my family this Christmas. Justice and closure."

"You'll do it," she said with absolute certainty. Thad Kendall was the kind of man who always succeeded in his goals. Too bad one of his goals was to remain single. "And you know you don't have to spend as much time around here as you do, if you'd rather be focusing on your investigation."

"Actually, I'd like to spend more time with Mark," he said. "I'd be happy to watch him during the day while you're at work."

"You want me to pull him out of day care?" She studied his handsome face through narrowed eyes, suspecting he had a reason other than just wanting to spend more time with his son.

He nodded. "I missed three years of his life. I'd like to get to know my son."

"I'll be off on my break in a few more days," she said. Because of the holiday fall-

ing on the weekend, she had only a half day
off the Friday before Christmas Eve, but she
didn't have to return until after New Year's
Day.

"But it's crazy for you to have to pay for
day care when I'm available to watch him,"
Thad persisted. The check he'd forced on her
earlier weakened his argument. He insisted
on paying for day care and all Mark's expenses.

Hell, he'd wanted to pay off her mortgage
and her car, too. But she'd never wanted his
money. What she wanted was much harder to
attain: his heart.

"Watch him or guard him?" she asked.

Now she wondered about all the time he'd
been spending with them since that night at
the mall. In the past week and a half, he'd
been over every day the minute she picked up
Mark from day care. "You really think he's
in danger?"

"Nothing's happened."

She nodded, clinging to the faint reassurance. "And you said that man at church was
your uncle."

"Sorry about that."

"He wanted to see his great-nephew," she

said. He had undoubtedly also wanted to check her out. He probably wondered what the heck Thad had ever seen in her. She wasn't a svelte socialite like Thad's mother had been; she was a real woman with real curves and damn proud of it.

"I need to bring you and Mark to Sunday dinner and have you meet the whole family," he said.

She heard the reluctance in his deep voice. "Need to—not *want* to."

He shrugged. "They can be overwhelming. Meeting all these new relatives at once might be a bit much for Mark."

She was touched that he had considered their son's feelings. "I think he'll like having a lot of family."

Thad chuckled. "They're all dying to meet him. Aunt Angela's been bugging me to get his Christmas list."

"He told Santa what he wanted for Christmas was family," she reminded him. "Sounds like he'll get it." With aunts and uncles, but not the family he really wanted—Mommy, Daddy and Mark.

"What do you want for Christmas?" she asked. "Besides your parents' killer brought to justice?"

He stepped closer, backing her against the wall. "You. I want you, Caroline."

He pressed his hips against hers, leaving her no doubt how much he wanted her. And he covered her mouth with his, parting her lips for the hot invasion of his tongue.

Her pulse quickened with desire. She wanted him, too. So much....

He lifted his head and implored her, his voice gruff with passion, "Let me stay tonight...."

To make love with her—or to protect her and Mark?

He touched her then—with his intense gaze and with his hands, sliding them down the sides of her breasts. His wet shirt had dampened hers, so that her hardened nipples were visible through the thin cotton. He groaned. "Caroline."

She wanted him to touch her there. She wanted him to touch her everywhere. She slid her arms around his shoulders and tangled her fingers in his soft hair, pulling his head down for another kiss.

"Be mine tonight," he urged her.

She was already his; she had been his for years. But he only wanted a night. She wanted forever. While she knew, intimately, how good making love with him was, she wanted more.

She forced herself to push him back. "You need to leave."

EVEN THE COLD NIGHT AIR blowing through his open coat to his still-damp T-shirt didn't cool Thad's desire. He wanted Caroline even more than he had four years ago, and four years ago he'd wanted her more than he had any other woman.

She was so beautiful and smart. And it was because she was smart that she refused to let him any closer. He didn't blame her, not after he'd hurt her before. Leaving her last time had been the hardest thing he'd ever done. To leave her and Mark this time…

Pain clutched his heart at just the thought. Then pain nipped his hand when he gripped the door handle. Blood streaked from his fingers, glass embedded in his skin.

In the glow of the streetlamp, his own reflection radiated back from the shattered window of his driver's door. The windshield was also broken. Hell, every damn window had been broken.

He ducked down, in case whoever had damaged the vehicle was still around, and he noted that all his tires were flat, the sidewalls slashed. While he'd been inside the house with Caroline and Mark, someone had been just outside, vandalizing his vehicle with such malice.

And maybe that person was still outside or, worse yet, trying to get inside the house. Out of reflex he reached beneath his jacket, but his gun wasn't there. That first night back, when he'd shot Natalie's stalker—her half brother—he'd had to use Gray's gun because he never tried to bring one through airport security. In other countries, he got his weapons through secret contacts. Fortunately, he had a couple contacts in St. Louis, too, but because he hadn't wanted to alarm Caroline, he'd left the gun in the glove box.

Of his vandalized car…

Keeping low, he dragged open the door and reached inside. Glass littered the dash and the seats. He got cut again as he fumbled for the glove box. His gun glinted in the darkness.

Maybe the vandal hadn't been inside his car. Or maybe he hadn't needed Thad's gun because he was already armed. With his free hand, Thad reached for his cell. He punched in a number and gave an address.

"Get here as fast as you can."

He had no intention of waiting for his backup, though, not when Caroline and Mark could be in danger. His gun clenched tight in his bleeding hand, he headed toward the house fully prepared to kill again. He would do anything to protect his family.

Chapter Nine

Caroline shivered with nerves and cold. If he hadn't flashed his badge, she wouldn't have let the man inside—not at this hour. He wasn't wearing a uniform or a suit but jeans and a wrinkled shirt that looked like he'd picked it up off the floor.

It was actually the name on the badge that had compelled her to unlock the door and let him inside: Detective Ash Kendall.

Cold air had rushed in with him. But what he'd told her had chilled her far more. "Thad's missing?"

"He called me—gave me your address and told me to get here right away," Ash said. "But he's gone."

"He just drove off?"

Ash shook his head. His hair wasn't as dark a brown as Thad's, and his eyes were green instead of blue, yet, from their guarded intensity, they were unmistakably brothers. "Not in *his* car."

"Why?" she asked. "Did something happen to it?"

Ash hesitated a moment as if deliberating how much to tell her. Then he admitted, "The tires have been slashed and all the windows broken."

"While it was sitting in my driveway?" she asked, horrified that someone dangerous had been that close to her home.

"He'd parked a ways down the street," Ash said. "But the car was under a light. Whoever did this was really bold."

Or really crazy.

"Where would Thad have gone?"

"I have a couple patrols looking for him," he said. "I'm sure he'll turn up. You know Thad…."

Did she? Sometimes she believed she knew him better than his own family did. But at times like now, when he disappeared, she wasn't sure anyone knew Thad—even Thad.

"But what if the person who did that to his car took him?" she asked.

"More likely Thad's trying to track down the vandal himself," Ash said. "And it was probably just a vandal. We've had reports in this area of malicious mischief—stolen or destroyed Christmas decorations, that kind of thing."

She glanced out the big picture window and shivered. "Someone knocked down all our snowmen…Mark's snow family."

From what she could see in the dim light falling from the picture window into the front yard, the snowmen hadn't been just knocked down but crushed. Even the snow boy. Mark would be devastated when he noticed that the snow family he'd built with his daddy was gone.

Ash let out a breath of relief. "Yeah, it's probably kids then, getting antsy for Christmas break."

"But to break windows and slash tires…" To Caroline, that felt more personal than a random act of vandalism.

"You're a teacher, right?" Ash asked.

She nodded. "Elementary school. None of my kids would do something like this."

"Well, kids don't stay that sweet and innocent nowadays," he warned her. "They egg each other on to bigger risks and greater violence."

"I know some high school teachers whose

houses have been egged and mailboxes knocked down," she admitted.

"Depending on where they teach, some have reported their cars stolen and themselves physically assaulted," he shared. "Even kids can be quite dangerous."

Caroline shuddered. "And Thad's out there by himself."

"We both know Thad's been in more dangerous places than a St. Louis suburb," Ash reminded her, "and he's come out without a scratch."

"I can't say the same now," a deep voice grumbled as Thad pushed open the door and stepped inside the living room. Blood dripped from a gash on his hand.

"Are you all right?" Caroline asked, her pulse tripping with fear.

His lips curved into a grim smile. "It's just a scratch."

"Looks like it might need stitches," Ash observed as he inspected the wound. "I wondered where all that blood had come from." He'd obviously been worried although he'd kept that information from Caroline.

She grabbed one of the Christmas stockings hanging from the fireplace and gently wrapped it around Thad's hand.

He groaned as he inspected the knitted reindeer-patterned stocking. "Yeah, that'll make it feel better."

"You need to stop the bleeding," she said, peeling back the stocking to look at the wound. "There could still be glass in the cut. You need to go to the emergency room and get this taken care of." She turned to his brother. "Why don't you take him?"

"No!" Thad said, his voice nearly a shout.

Ash shook his head. "She's right. It looks bad."

"I don't need to go," Thad said with a pointed stare at his older brother.

The detective nodded with sudden understanding of their nonverbal exchange. "Caroline could take you, and I could stay here."

"No," she said, rejecting the idea. "I don't want Mark to wake up with a stranger."

"He's his uncle," Thad said.

"Who he's never met," she reminded him. "He's a stranger, and after the incident at the mall, I put the fear of God in Mark about strangers. There's no way I could leave him alone with one."

Thad sighed. "You're right."

"So I'll take you then?" Ash asked tentatively.

With a grimace, Thad tied the Christmas stocking around his hand. "I don't need to go. It'll be fine."

Ash glanced out the window. "I need to go. Looks like the department tow truck is here."

"Department tow truck?" Thad asked.

"Yeah, we'll bring your car in," the SLPD detective said, "and see if we can find any fingerprints or anything on it."

"But you said it was probably just kids," Caroline reminded him. The brothers' intensity unnerved her; something was going on.

Ash nodded. "More than likely, since they took out the snow *family,* too."

Thad glanced out the front window at the desecrated snowmen he'd made with his son, and a muscle twitched along his tightly clenched jaw. "I'll go out to the tow truck with you," Thad said.

Caroline stepped closer, worried about more than his hand now. "But you're hurt—"

"I'll see that he takes care of it," Ash promised. "And it was nice to finally meet you. I'd like to meet your son—" his throat moved as he swallowed "—my nephew, too."

"Sunday dinner," Thad said. "She and Mark are going to come to Sunday dinner."

"But Sunday's…"

Christmas. Thad hadn't realized, nor had he obviously intended to invite her home for Christmas. She'd actually forgotten, too.

"We'll see you Sunday then," Ash continued with excitement. "It'll be great to have a little one around to open up presents. It just might make Christmas special again."

Thad said nothing, neither taking back nor confirming his invitation. He just opened the door for his brother and then followed him out. The door had barely shut behind them when she heard them raise their voices in an argument.

From the look on Thad's face, she doubted that she and Mark would be showing up on Sunday. She also doubted that Christmas would ever be special again for the Kendalls.

"WHAT THE HELL is the matter with you?" Ash yelled. "Why'd you go running after some malicious vandals unarmed?" He grabbed at Thad, patting the bulge under his jacket. "You're not unarmed. What the hell are you?"

"Prepared," he lied.

He hadn't been prepared at all, so it was good that he hadn't actually found anything more frightening than a half-frozen raccoon in the little alley behind Caroline's house. He hadn't even noticed that Mark's snow family had been destroyed. As he stared at the trampled mounds of snow on her front yard, his gut clenched with regret and anger. That bothered him more than the damage to his car.

Whoever had done all this had been so damn close to the house.

If only he'd looked out the window and caught him. But instead he'd been giving Mark a bath and then trying to seduce Caroline into bed.

"Where and how did you get a gun?" Ash persisted.

"I'm not entirely without connections in this town," he reminded his older brother.

Ash shuddered. "You don't need the kind of connections that'll hook you up with a gun," he said. "You need to focus on your connections in that house—that woman and your son."

"That's why I needed the gun," Thad admitted. "To protect them."

Ash's green eyes narrowed with suspicion. "What makes you so damn certain that they need protecting?"

He gestured at his damaged car and what had once been Mark's snow family. "This…"

"It could have been vandals, like I told her," Ash said. "The suburbs have been getting hit hard this holiday."

"And Mark nearly getting abducted at the mall?"

"Could have been the mistake the security guards thought it—"

"Why didn't whoever grabbed him bring him back to his mother then?" Thad said. "I thought you, out of everyone, wouldn't be so damn naive and trusting anymore."

Ash grabbed Thad's jacket, his face tight with concern and impatience. "And why the hell are you so damn untrusting? Has there been a threat against you?" He glanced back at the house, where Caroline watched them through the front window. "Against them?"

Thad shook his head. "But my gut's telling me they're in danger."

Ash sighed. "I'd put a car out front, but I need more than your windows shattered and your tires slashed to warrant around-the-clock protection. The best I can do is step up patrols in the neighborhood. I'll send a car past every hour or so."

Ignoring the pain in his wounded hand, Thad grabbed Ash's shoulders and squeezed. "Thanks. It'll help until I can convince Caroline to move her and Mark on to the estate with me."

"You think the estate is safe?" Ash asked.

Given everything that had happened there, in the distant past and not so distant past when Natalie and Gray had nearly died at the cottage on the grounds, Thad couldn't claim that it was. "I just want them with me."

"And she won't let you stay here?" His brother gestured at the brick Cape Cod.

"She doesn't trust me," Thad admitted.

"So she's as smart as she is beautiful," Ash remarked with a grin.

"Hey!"

"I don't trust you, either, little brother," Ash admitted. "I think you've been keeping bigger secrets than her and your son from us."

Just then Thad's cell rang, with the distinctive tone that indicated it was his boss, his *real* boss, calling. "I've gotta take this," he said, stepping back as the tow driver approached Ash.

While his brother was busy with the department employee, he walked farther down the block to get out of Ash's hearing, and Caroline's if she came out of the house. "Kendall," he answered the call.

"I got a message that you needed to speak to me immediately," Anya said.

He had called her after he'd called Ash.

"What's wrong?" she asked.

"I think Michaels gave me up," he said. "I think the wrong people have found out who I really am."

"Has there been an attempt on your life?" she asked, her voice full of concern.

"No." He glanced down at his hand. "But something happened—someone's trying to send me a message." And he had received it loud and clear. He and his family were not safe in St. Louis.

"What happened?" she asked.

When he told her, she made no reply. "I know it doesn't sound serious, but I'd like some protection."

"You would?" she asked, her voice sharp with surprise.

"Not for me," he admitted. "I discovered something recently." Something that had changed everything for him.

"Your parents' killer?" she asked. "That's good. Then you can come back in now. I've been holding an assignment that requires your special skills."

"To finish the assignment with Michaels

and find his killer?" He had always assumed that would be his next job.

She made a noise like a pen clicking or gun cocking. One never knew with Anya. "That assignment is no longer a priority."

"A man died—"

"I need you for something more important. When will you be ready to return?"

"I haven't found my parents' killer yet," he said. But maybe, if he hadn't been compromised, the killer had found him. "I found out that I have a son."

"You're a father?" she asked, shock clear in the sharp crack of her voice.

"Yes. He's three years old, and someone tried to grab him from the mall a couple weeks ago. And tonight vandalism happened outside his house. I think someone's threatening my son." And his mother. "To get to me."

A sigh of heavy disappointment rattled the phone. "If you were compromised, no one would know that you had a son," she pointed out. "This has nothing to do with what you do for your country."

"So you won't help me protect my family?" After all the years he had cared nothing of his own safety, putting his life on the line, to protect others?

"I can't misappropriate manpower when there's been no obvious threat," she told him, clicking off the call as if she cared to hear nothing else he had to say.

And given that he had revealed himself to be as much a liability as Michaels, maybe she didn't care anymore.

He glanced up to find his brother watching him, his eyes narrowed with suspicion. Detective Kendall hadn't considered the damage here tonight a threat, either. Maybe it wasn't obvious to him or to Agent Anya Smith, but it was obvious to Thad that his family had been threatened.

SLASHING THE TIRES, breaking the windows, destroying the snow *family*—Ed had done it all in a fit of fury. Even now, hours later, his heart pounded erratically over the risk he'd taken.

He could have been caught, and then it all would have been over before he'd had a chance to mete out the punishment that Thad Kendall deserved.

But he'd had to wait too long to dole out that punishment. And while he bided his time—the most opportune time—to grab the boy, Thad Kendall got to play happy family.

But he had caught a glimpse of Thad's face tonight, when the man had discovered the damage to his car, and Kendall hadn't been happy. He'd been scared, not for himself but for them. He knew for certain that they were in danger now.

Sure, it would make him even more vigilant, more determined than ever to protect them. But then, when he failed, and Ed would see to it that he failed miserably, it would hurt him even more. Because there was no worse feeling than failing those you loved....

Chapter Ten

"Are you okay?" Tammy asked, tapping her knuckles against Caroline's open classroom door. The children had gone down to lunch. Usually Caroline would have been with Tammy in the teacher's lounge by now, eating her own lunch.

She nodded, but her head pounded with the movement. She hadn't managed to get much sleep the night before, even after Thad and his brother had left her house. And every time she'd glanced out her window, she'd noticed a St. Louis Police Department patrol car driving past. Instead of the police presence reassuring her, it had made her more uneasy.

"I'm not sure," she replied honestly.

"Things not going well with Thad?" Tammy asked, her voice soft with sympathy.

"He's great with Mark," she admitted. "So patient and sweet."

"You sound surprised. Or disappointed?"

Caroline leaned back in her chair and sighed. "Maybe both."

Tammy chuckled. "I understand."

"How can you when I don't?" Caroline wondered.

"After we had kids and I saw what a great father Steve is, I fell deeper in love with him, deeper than I'd thought it possible to love anyone," Tammy shared.

"I can't love Thad," Caroline insisted.

"Why not?"

"Besides the whole leaving thing," Caroline said, "there's also the fact that I don't trust him. He's keeping something from me and his family, something important." Something that might have put their son in danger.

"Like another wife and kid?" Tammy asked.

She shook her head. "Something dangerous."

"Sure, he puts himself in danger when he goes to those countries to report on war," Tammy allowed. "But he's home now. What danger could he be in?"

Caroline flashed back to his car with the shattered windows and slashed tires. And Mark's poor, crushed snow family. Her little boy had been devastated when he'd seen the snowmen gone that morning. She'd promised him that Thad would come back and help him rebuild them even bigger.

But was it wise for Thad to be around his son if he was in danger? Maybe he hadn't brought the danger back with him from whatever war-torn country he'd been in last. Maybe the danger had been waiting for Thad to come home all along.

"His parents were murdered here," she reminded Tammy.

"The Christmas Eve Murders, everyone knows that," Tammy replied with a shudder of revulsion. She much preferred romance to reality. "That happened twenty years ago."

"But the man they'd thought had killed the parents wasn't the real killer."

Tammy nodded. "I know. My husband works for the news, remember?"

"I'm sorry—"

"You're scared," her friend observed, "about more than just falling for Thad Kendall all over again, too."

"Yes, I am. That killer—the real killer—is still out there, you know." And had he been out there the night before in her front yard, destroying the snowman family her son had made with his father?

Tammy shook her head. "No, you don't know that. Twenty years have passed. He could have died."

"But what if he didn't?"

Her friend shrugged off her concerns. "If I got away with murder, I would have gotten the hell out of town."

"But now, with the other man cleared, he didn't get away with it."

"Even more reason to stay far, far away from St. Louis," Tammy said. "Criminals very rarely return to the scenes of their crimes."

Caroline blew out a breath of relief. "You're right."

"So are you going to come eat now?" Tammy asked. "I brought salads for today, so we can pig out tomorrow when everyone brings something for our Christmas lunch."

Caroline's stomach growled, more at the mention of the Christmas lunch than the salad. But before she could stand up, her cell rang. She opened her bottom drawer, pulled out her purse and then her phone.

"It's the day care," she said. "I have to take this."

"I hope Mark's all right," Tammy said.

"I'm sure he is." This was probably about Thad. Had he shown up and tried to take Mark out despite her telling him not to?

"Have them give Bethany a hug from Mommy for me," Tammy said, referring to her daughter, who was in the same day care. Then she headed out the door, off to her salad.

"Hello," she said. "This is Caroline Emerson."

"Hi, Caroline," the day care director said.

"Is Mark all right?"

"Yes, yes, all the children are all right. But I felt I needed to call and let you know…"

Caroline's heart rate quickened with the nerves in the director's voice. "What?"

"There was a man hanging around earlier. He never approached the center or the children," the director assured her, "but he was standing around outside as if he was watching the place."

"Was he about thirty?" Caroline asked. "Good-looking with brown hair and blue eyes?"

The director chuckled. "No, it wasn't Mark's father."

"You know who Mark's father is?"

"Thad Kendall," the director said then sputtered, "but he didn't tell us that. He came by earlier with his brother, Detective Ash Kendall, and Mark called him Daddy."

"Thanks for letting me know that he came by," Caroline said.

And he'd brought Ash, too?

"He asked that we call him or his brother if we saw anything suspicious around the day care," the woman continued. "If he hadn't stopped by today and said that very thing, we might not have thought anything of that man standing outside. This is a busy area after all, so it's not unusual that someone stand outside the coffee shop across the street waiting for someone."

So Thad's suspicious nature had unsettled them, too.

"That's why I'm not certain we should even call them about the man," the director continued. "We may just be overreacting. He was an older gentleman and very well dressed. I'm sure he was just waiting to meet someone."

"No," Caroline said. "You should call them about it. Actually, just call Detective Kendall. He'll know whether it's anything to worry about."

Or just his brother's paranoia.

Why was Thad so certain that their son was in danger?

What the hell was he keeping from her?

HE WAS LOSING HIS MIND. Ash had told him as much, and so had Caroline. He had panicked when she and Mark hadn't been home after work. She hadn't appreciated his calling while she and their son were at her friend's house baking cookies for the Christmas parties at both her school and Mark's day care.

Needless to say, she hadn't invited him to join them despite her friend, in the background, shouting out an invitation. He smiled at Tammy Stehouwer's obvious matchmaking. The woman had been right, though, that he and Caroline would hit it off. They had four years ago.

And if Caroline would give him a chance, they would again. But she wasn't about to give him a chance, not until he was ready to tell her everything. No one deserved the burden of knowing everything about his life, about the things he'd seen and done. But he wasn't at liberty to reveal the things he'd seen and done or even what he really was. He would lose his job for certain and maybe even his life, given that the people he'd spied on were usually prone to vengeance.

But Caroline, being Caroline with her big heart and her maternal instincts, had assured him that she and Mark were safe. They were spending the night at Tammy's, and Steve Stehouwer had already turned on the security system.

Thad would have to trust that they were safe for the night. So, ready to give in to the need for the sleep he'd been denying his body, he climbed the stairs to his and his siblings' wing of the house. His was the only occupied suite at the moment. Ash and Devin had their own places, and Natalie had officially moved in with Gray. Guilt and regret tugged at him.

Did she not feel as if she belonged on the Kendall estate since she wasn't biologically a Kendall? Or did she just need the comfort and protection of her fiancé now? Thad would call her in the morning to make certain she was all right. She had acted so tough when he'd told her the truth. But maybe she'd only been acting.

Yawning, he reached the door to his suite and pushed it open, using his bandaged hand. Despite his protests, Ash had taken him to the emergency room last night and had his wound flushed out. He'd forgone the stitches and could probably lose the bandage when he showered. It hadn't been as bad as Caroline and Ash had worried it was.

He'd been hurt far worse than that before. And probably would again if he ignored his instincts. They were niggling at him now. His door hadn't been shut tight.

But maybe Aunt Angela had had someone clean the room today, which would have been kind of pointless when he'd actually spent so little time in it. Ever since the incident at the mall, he'd spent most nights in his car outside Caroline's house.

Maybe that was why his windows had been smashed, so that he couldn't spend the night protecting them. His guts tightened with fear and anger; someone was definitely after his son.

He stepped forward and in the semidarkness of the room, tripped over something on the floor. Whoever had cleaned up had done a half-assed job. He cursed and fumbled along the wall for the light switch. The lamp came on, but it wasn't sitting on the bedside table. Instead, it lay on the floor, its shade bent and the base cracked.

It wasn't the only thing broken in the room.

Like his window, the mirror above the dresser was smashed, all the toiletries swept to the floor. And the photo albums that he'd borrowed from the library were strewn across the floor, the pictures torn or crumpled with the same rage that someone had destroyed his car and Mark's snow family.

Someone had been inside his room. Inside the house, just like they had the night his parents had been murdered. Natalie was gone. But Uncle Craig and Aunt Angela would be home.

He reached for the gun that he'd tucked into the waistband of his jeans. And, with his weapon drawn, he stalked around his own house as if he were in another country checking for insurgents.

His wing was empty. The first floor was deserted, too. So he headed up the stairs to the other wing of the house, where Aunt Angela and Uncle Craig used the master suite that had once been his parents'…until they had been murdered there.

The house looked nothing like it had before their deaths. As if to erase their memories of that horrible time, Aunt Angela had redecorated the whole house. While it was elegant, it was also as warm and vibrant as the woman herself.

His heart thudded in his throat as he approached the French doors to the bedroom where his parents' bodies had been found.

Where they'd been murdered.

His gun clutched tight in his bandaged hand, he pushed open the doors. And a scream rent the air.

Aunt Angela pressed her hand against her heart, which was dangerous as she held a pair of scissors. She'd been wrapping presents on the bed. "What are you doing?"

With a sigh of relief, Thad lowered the barrel of his gun. "Are you all right?"

She nodded. "Except for the ten years you scared off my life."

He glanced around the bedroom. "Where's Uncle Craig?"

"At work yet," she replied, hurt dimming some of the usual warmth of her brown eyes. "He's been working a lot lately." She focused on the gun again. "What are you doing with that? What happened to your hand?"

"I'm okay," he assured her.

"What's going on?"

"Someone's been in the house," he said. Pitching his voice low, he added, "They could still be here." He grabbed his phone, but instead of punching in Ash's number, he dialed 911. He needed the closest available unit for backup.

After dropping the scissors atop the unwound roll of paper, Aunt Angela reached out for his hand, hers shaking. "Stay with me."

"Of course." After pushing aside the wrapping stuff, he settled beside her on the bed. It wasn't the same bed where his parents had been murdered but it brought back those same horrific memories.

She squeezed his hand. "I'm sorry."

"What are you sorry about?" he wondered. His aunt had never done anything wrong.

"I thought it was all over for you—that the man who'd gone to prison was the killer. I thought we were all safe here." She shivered. "But I was wrong. He's back, isn't he?"

He'd thought the threat might have come from someone from his other life, from another country—but not now.

"Yeah, he's back."

And he was proving to them that he could still get inside the house as easily as he had the night he had killed Joseph and Marie Kendall.

He shivered, too.

"How do you know *he* was here?" she asked, trembling as she glanced around her room as if remembering that it had once been a crime scene.

"He was in my suite," Thad said. "I'm surprised and very glad that you didn't hear him." If Aunt Angela had heard anything and gone to investigate... Thad blocked out the images of everything that could have happened to her. "He really tossed the place."

"I left this morning after the cleaning staff had been here, and then I was gone all afternoon," she said. "Christmas shopping. I just got back a little while ago."

"Maybe he waited until after you'd left to break in." Maybe he hadn't wanted to hurt Angela Kendall. Thad glanced around his aunt's room again, which was untouched, as was the rest of the house. Maybe he was the only Kendall this guy wanted to hurt.

He remembered the pictures then. "I should have put those albums back right after I looked through them." Because now they were destroyed.

"We can figure out a way to replace pictures," she assured him. "We can't replace family."

"You did," he said, so grateful that she

hadn't been harmed and so grateful for what she'd done for him and his siblings. "You were a better mother to us than she ever was."

"Thad," she gasped at his pronouncement. "You shouldn't say that."

"The truth?" He wrapped his arm around her. "It is the truth. You were always there for us, like she never was."

"Your mother was so beautiful," Aunt Angela murmured wistfully. "And your father was so driven. She needed attention."

"And when she didn't get it from him, where did she get it?" If anyone knew, it was Aunt Angela. While she and his mother hadn't had much in common, they had been family, if not friends.

She shook her head. "I can't speak ill of her."

"Because she's dead?" He'd never understood that. Since the person was already dead, what did it matter if anyone spoke ill of them?

"Because she was your mother," she said, "and you should have only good memories of her."

"She was pretty and she always smelled nice," Thad said. "That's what I remember about her. You're the one who came to all our sports events and school plays and pageants. You're the one who made us dinner every night and baked us cookies."

Tears streaked from her eyes, which she squeezed shut. "Oh, you were always the charmer, Thad Kendall."

"I realize that you're trying to protect me from the truth about my mother," he said, loving her for her sensitivity, "but I need the truth so that I can protect this family from a killer."

She sighed wistfully. "Your mother was so beautiful and charming. You get your charm from her. I used to think she might have been just a flirt…."

Thad shook his head. "A friend of Devin's worked at a hotel where she used to meet some guy. Or guys."

"Your mother flirted a lot," she said, "especially at the company functions we attended before your uncle and I moved to California." After their son had died in that tragic auto accident, Craig had sold his half of Kendall Communications to his older brother, who he'd known would have never let him have any real control of the company.

"So you think the guy—or guys—may have actually worked for Dad?"

"Marie liked to be flattered," Angela said. "And no one is as good at flattering someone as a salesman."

"So Mom liked the salesmen at Kendall Communications?"

Aunt Angela nodded. "Yes. At every company function, they fought for her attention, jumping around like puppies and bringing her drinks. But I don't know what ones it might have gone beyond flirting with."

"Ones?"

She drew in a deep breath and finally uttered a few names, which Thad had her jot down on a piece of her floral stationery. "They were the good-looking ones," she said as she passed him the paper. "The ones she actually seemed interested in, too."

"Did any of them have a son named Wade?"

She shrugged. "Twenty years was a long time ago."

Sometimes. And sometimes, as the anniversary of their murders approached, it seemed like just hours ago. He could remember the crime-scene techs and detectives all descended on his house, like they probably would be soon.

"I don't remember their kids' names," she

said. "I barely remembered their names—just thought of one when your brother Devin mentioned him a few days ago."

"Devin mentioned him?"

She shrugged. "Something about business…"

So maybe some of them still worked for Kendall Communications. "I'll call Devin and have him check company records. They would have had their kids listed as dependents on tax and insurance documents."

He would have him check not just sons named Wade but any in the approximate age bracket. Thad reached for his phone again, but as he did, the bedroom doors burst open, and he was the one staring down the barrel of a gun.

This time his brother's.

Aunt Angela gasped and touched her heart again. "You boys…"

"I heard the call come over the radio," Ash said. "What the hell's going on now?"

"Check out my rooms," Thad ordered him. "They were vandalized like my car."

Ash looked from him to Aunt Angela, who'd gone deathly pale. "Are you both okay?"

Thad nodded and assured him, "I'll stay with Auntie."

"I'm fine," she said shakily as Ash rushed off to search the rest of the house.

Thad could have told him he'd already done that, but he figured a detective wouldn't trust a reporter to have done a thorough job. Even an armed reporter.

"We'll just stay here until Uncle Craig gets home." He was sure that Ash would call him, too, if he hadn't already.

"I'm sorry," she said, laying her head on his shoulder. "I should have told you about your mother earlier."

"You were trying to protect us," Thad said. "I understand that."

She patted his hand. "You do, now that you have your own son. I lost mine…." Her breath audibly caught. "But then I got all of you. And you became my children. I would do anything to protect you, like you will Mark."

"I will," he agreed.

But what he'd realized when he'd found the damage in his room was that the best way for him to protect Mark was to let him go.

Chapter Eleven

The beeping of a breaking news bulletin drew Caroline's attention to the television in the teacher's lounge. She stepped away from the buffet table of goodies where everyone had congregated and walked over to the TV, which flashed an image of the infamous Kendall estate behind the female anchor.

"Police were called to the Kendall mansion last night, just days before the twenty-year anniversary of the Christmas Eve Murders of Joseph and Marie Kendall."

Tammy gasped and grasped Caroline's arm in silent support. "Steve took off this week and next so he could spend the holidays with me and the kids, so I didn't know about this yet."

Otherwise she knew her friend would have warned her. Why hadn't Thad warned her? Or at least called to assure her that he was all right? Because they weren't the happy family Mark—and she—wanted them to be.

Caroline shook off her flash of pain and focused on the anchor's report.

"The Kendall family would not make an official statement to the police, but an inside source confirms that acclaimed photojournalist Thad Kendall called 911 to report a break-in at the estate."

The woman smiled at the mention of Thad but then pulled her face back into a serious mask. "Could it be that the killer, who authorities just learned in the last few months is free, has returned to the scene of his crime?"

Tammy reached up and shut off the television. "That's ridiculous," she said. "There have been a lot of break-ins lately. There always is around Christmastime but given the poor economy, there are even more this year."

Caroline nodded, but she felt sick, the sweets she'd eaten rising up in her throat. Ignoring the party, she rushed out into the quiet hallway. The children had already been dismissed at noon to begin their Christmas break.

"He's okay," Tammy said as she followed

her out. "They would have said had anyone been hurt."

Caroline nodded again. "I know."

But she wasn't worried about just Thad. She hurried into her classroom, dug her cell out of her purse and punched in the number for the day care.

"This is Caroline Emerson," she said. "Is Mark all right?"

The young assistant, who had picked up, laughed. "He's having a great time. We're playing games and eating the cookies you and Mrs. Stehouwer brought this morning."

Regret tugged at Caroline but she said, "I'm going to pick him up in just a few minutes."

Tammy had followed her into her classroom. "Let Steve do it," she said. "He already picked up Steve Jr. from his half day of school, and he's picking up Bethany from day care in just a few minutes."

"But I can—"

"You have company," Tammy said, stepping back to allow Thad into the room. In jeans and a leather jacket, he was as sexy as ever.

Caroline clenched her hand around her phone, so that she wouldn't throw it down and run to wrap her arms around his neck. What if he'd been injured or worse during the break-in?

"Okay." She focused on her call. "Uh, Mr. Stehouwer will be picking up Mark today along with his daughter."

That was good. Mark would be safe with Steve.

She was the one in danger now…because Thad didn't look like the man who had built a snow family with their son and who had held her throughout the night. He looked as cold and distant as the man who'd walked away from her without a backward glance four years ago.

"I'll call Steve and let him know he's picking up Mark, too. We'll be happy to watch him until you come to pick him up," Tammy generously offered as she pulled shut the door to the classroom, leaving Caroline alone with Thad. If she'd been hoping to play matchmaker again, she was going to be disappointed.

But not nearly as disappointed as Caroline was sure she was going to be. She dropped into the chair behind her desk. "Why are you here?" she asked. "Has something happened…something *else?*"

"You heard about the break-in," he surmised.

"You should have called me." Heat rushed to her face. "For Mark's sake," she hastened to explain. "If he's in danger…"

IF THEIR SON WAS IN DANGER, it was because of Thad, so the best way to keep him and Caroline safe was to keep his distance from them.

"This was a bad idea," Thad said, forcing out the words. He couldn't look at her, so he gazed around her classroom instead. The walls served as sunshine-yellow backdrops for the kids' colorful artwork and starred papers.

"What was?" she asked, as if bracing herself for the worst.

"My trying to be a father." He swallowed hard, choking on the lies. "You were right that I'm not cut out for it."

She sucked in a breath of surprise, but she didn't argue with him. He had hoped she would argue, that she would tell him he was better at being a dad than he had thought he could be.

He had been so worried that he would have already done or said something to screw up his relationship with Mark and make the little boy hate him. But he was pretty sure his son loved him as much as Thad loved Mark. And it was because Thad loved him so much that he had to back away.

But if he told Caroline the truth, she might argue with him. She might think, as his brother had and she had earlier, that he was just overreacting and being paranoid. She might convince him to stay in his son's life instead of his convincing her that it was best he stay away from Mark.

The sad thing was that she seemed to need no convincing. Caroline said nothing, just stared up at him with dry eyes. It was as if she'd cried herself out over him four years ago and didn't intend to waste any more tears on him.

He didn't blame her. "I should have just stayed away from him and you," he said. "I'll be leaving soon anyways."

"You will?" she asked, her voice barely above a whisper.

He jerked his head in a sharp nod.

"You found your parents' killer?"

"Not yet," he admitted. "But we're pretty sure we're closing in on him now."

Yesterday he had only glanced over the names his aunt had written down, thinking that he wouldn't have recognized any of them since he'd just been a kid when his parents died. But when he'd studied the list more closely, one name had jumped out at him.

Ed Turner.

When he'd questioned Aunt Angela about him, she'd been unable to say for certain that his mother had had an affair with the man. But she'd admitted that the two had always looked at each other a certain way, as if they'd seen more of each other. A lot more of each other.

"So you know who their killer is?"

He sighed. "We don't have any proof yet." Of the affair or anything else. Hell, they hadn't even been able to find Turner yet. Devin had been trying to track down the man for months in order to extend an offer for his company.

And it was the man's disappearance that worried Thad. A lot of what he'd learned about Ed Turner worried him, and had made him Thad's prime suspect even though his brothers weren't as convinced of the man's guilt.

"Are the police looking at him as a suspect, too?" she asked.

A respected businessman whose company

held several defense contracts for communications equipment? He would be their last
suspect. But Thad's gut told him otherwise.

"We'll find the evidence with or without
the police department's help." He would get
Turner's DNA himself, court order or sub-
poena be damned. He just had to find Turner,
in order to keep everyone Thad cared about
safe.

"So as soon as whoever this guy is has
been arrested, you'll be leaving?"

He nodded. "You've known that all along."

She surprised him with a laugh. "Wow.
Here's déjà vu for you."

"We have had this conversation before."
And it was almost as hard this time as it had
been last time. But this time he was leaving
for her sake and Mark's. To protect them.

She sighed. "And I knew we'd be having it
again."

"That's why you didn't want me getting
close to you," he said. "You were right about
that. I shouldn't have tried to get close to
Mark, either. Hopefully he's not too attached
to me that he'll miss me when I'm gone."

"You haven't been around that long," she
said, as if implying that Mark would forget
about him.

Pain clutched Thad's heart. Would his son forget all about him? At three, he was young enough to do that. But Thad wasn't going to stay away forever, just until the threat against his son was gone.

But given the way Thad lived, would the threat against him ever really be gone?

"This is for the best," he said, trying to convince himself. "I'm not father material. You and Mark will be better off."

"With you halfway across the world? With you putting your life in danger?"

"It's what I do."

She nodded, and her eyes shimmered with tears. "We will be better off if you leave now," she agreed. "Because you're going to leave eventually anyways. For good, when you get killed because you put yourself in the middle of someone else's war."

Someone else's war.

Was that what he'd been fighting, someone else's war, when he should have been fighting his own here at home? Of course no one had known then that the wrong man had been convicted of his parents' murders.

"What I do is important," he defended himself.

She nodded. "And if you didn't do it, someone else would. It doesn't have to be you. But you'd rather go off alone to those countries and let someone else raise your son."

She hadn't married in the past four years, but Thad wasn't arrogant enough to believe that was because she'd been in love with him. She'd just been totally focused on raising their son. But when Mark got older, she would find someone. That nine-to-five guy she deserved.

Pain clutched his heart. "Caroline…"

She shook her head. "It's fine. I didn't expect anything from you. Unfortunately, Mark did. But I'll tell him…" She sucked in a shaky breath. "You don't have to see him again." She stood, as if prepared to show him out the door. "And I don't have to see you again, either."

He turned for the door, walking slowly in case she changed her mind and tried to stop him. But he would never know if she would have because her cell phone rang. He opened the door, ready to leave her just as he had planned.

But she cried out, "No!"

His heart leaped against his ribs, and he whirled back around to her. "What's happened?"

Her face had paled, and she trembled uncontrollably, the cell phone dropping from her hand onto her desk. "A man with a gun stormed the day care."

Oh, God. God, no...

He fought down the fear. "Was anyone hurt?"

"Tammy's husband," she whispered. "Steve tried to stop the man, and he was shot."

"And Mark?" What had happened to their sweet little boy?

Her eyes widened with horror and filled with tears. "The man took him."

BLOOD SPATTERED THE little boy's face, and red streaks trailed down his cheeks with tears. His hand shaking slightly, Ed wiped a damp washcloth across the kid's skin and washed away the blood.

It wasn't the boy's blood. He hadn't been hurt. Yet.

"It's not real?" the kid asked, his bottom lip trembling.

"It's fake," Ed lied. "That man wasn't really hurt. We were just playing a game. Like cops and robbers, you know."

The little boy's breath shuddered out in a ragged sigh of relief. "Mommy doesn't let me play cops and robbins. She says it's too vi'lin." He shivered. "And it was a really scary game."

"Sometimes adults play scary games," Ed said. And then, inevitably, someone got hurt. Too bad that this time it would be this little boy.

"So you know Bethany's daddy?"

Even though he had only recognized Steve Stehouwer because he was the anchor on the local news, Ed nodded. The man shouldn't have tried to play hero, and he wouldn't have gotten shot. But there were always innocent casualties in war. And when Thad Kendall had killed his son, he had declared war on Ed Turner. Kendall wasn't the only one who'd spent years dodging bullets and roadside bombs in foreign countries. After he'd left his cushy sales job at Kendall Communications, Turner had launched his own company specializing in defense communications. In order to meet the needs of his clients, he'd walked in their shoes. He'd lived as a spy. That was why he had immediately recognized Thad Kendall for what he really was.

A killer.

Ed led the little boy out of the dated pink-and-lime-green bathroom into the kitchen. He didn't trust the kid in the living room where he might turn on the TV and learn from the news that Ed had lied about the game. The kid would find out soon enough that this was very real.

"Are you related to *my* daddy?" the little boy asked as he settled onto a chair at the old Formica table. His blue eyes wide, he stared at the pictures of his father and him and his mother plastered all over the walls. "Mommy says he has a big family."

"Yes, he does. And I guess that in a way I am related to him," Ed said as he took the box of hot chocolate packets out of the cupboard. He could at least make the little kid comfortable while he waited to implement the next phase of his plan. If only he could make himself comfortable with a damn strong drink.… "I'm your aunt Natalie's father."

The little boy peered through the doorway into the living room and then turned toward the open door of the bathroom off the hall. "Is Aunt Natalie here?"

"No." Natalie had never really been his. Her paternity had been denied and covered up so that Marie Kendall wouldn't lose what she'd valued most. Money. Image. Her looks.

In the end she'd lost them all. Just as her son Thad would. He had been the last of her

Daddy Bombshell

children by Joseph Kendall, and although he hadn't joined the business, he was still the most like him.

Ruthless. Determined to keep what he considered his...even when it had really belonged to Ed.

Like Natalie.

And Marie.

But Ed wasn't as upset over losing them as he was over losing his son. His boy had stood by him through it all and had died trying to protect him. Ed hadn't deserved his boy's loyalty. He hadn't been a good father to Wade.

After Marie had refused to accept Ed's offer to leave Emily and build a life with her, Ed had quit Kendall. He'd started his own company, intent on making it even bigger than Joseph had. He hadn't. But he'd built a strong niche company, and in those war-torn countries, he'd learned what was really important.

Emily. She had always been so loving and supportive, uncomplaining when he was never around, never telling him how much their son had suffered. How much she had suffered. He'd intended to make it up to her that night, but then he and his family had run into the Kendalls at a holiday charity function.

He'd seen Natalie and known immediately she was his daughter…and what he'd been denied. He'd only intended to talk to Marie when he'd used his key to let himself into her house later that night. But things had gone so wrong.

Emily had never figured out what had happened. She'd claimed to understand that he had to keep traveling for his job. He had never been able to stop traveling, because he'd worried that even though another man had been convicted, he would eventually be caught. But the only one who'd figured out his guilt was his son, even though it had taken him years to piece it all together. And still Wade had stood by him.

He deserved to have his death avenged. Ed owed him that much since he'd never been there for his son, just as Thad Kendall had never been there for his son.

Ed drew in a deep breath and reached for the block of knives on the kitchen counter. It was just too bad that to avenge Wade, Ed would have to take the life of this sweet kid.

Chapter Twelve

Caroline had thought her heart had hurt during Thad's callous goodbye speech. But she hadn't known how much a heart could rip apart until the day care director had called to report Mark missing, taken by an armed gunman.

She couldn't stop shaking. And it didn't help that she was here, at the Kendall mansion, where people had been murdered, perhaps by the same man who'd abducted her son and shot her friend.

While Thad had filled in his family on what had happened at the day care center, she had phoned Tammy and had been surprised her friend had even taken her call. But Tammy, being the friend she was, had been as concerned about Mark as she was her own wounded husband. Steve was still in surgery, having a bullet removed from his shoulder. The doctors had assured Tammy that the gunshot wound was not life-threatening. Steve Stehouwer would live.

But she had no such assurances about her son.

Strong arms wrapped around her, pulling her back against a chest in which a heart pounded as madly as hers did.

"We'll find him," Thad assured her.

She tugged free of his grasp and whirled on him. "How? You're not even certain who took him!"

His family, who had all gathered in the family room, grew quiet and watched her, probably afraid she was losing her mind. But what did she care? If she'd truly lost her son, what did losing her mind matter?

Ash, the only one of Thad's family she had previously met, approached them. The St. Louis PD detective said, "We have a lead on the man who murdered our parents."

"But why would he take Mark?" she asked. "Why would he come after *my* son?"

"Money," Craig Kendall, the man she'd seen at St. Luke's, remarked. "He may call us with a demand for ransom so that he can get to some country with no extradition."

He thought like a businessman—logically.

She thought like a mother, and so did the woman who approached her. She had to be the aunt Thad had spoken of so lovingly. She folded Caroline into her arms as if she were one of the family.

"We'll pay whatever he asks," she promised. "We'll get our Mark back."

Our. They'd already claimed her son as a Kendall. She clutched at the woman's softness and warmth before pulling back.

Tears streamed down her face, but she couldn't fight them back any longer. "We don't know that this is about ransom or revenge," she pointed out. "We don't know the whole story because Thad won't tell us."

Instead of staring at her as if she'd lost her mind, Thad's family was staring at him. All of them with the same suspicion and doubt that she'd harbored.

He shook his head. "We don't have time for this. I have calls to make—"

"To whom?" his oldest brother asked. "That mysterious woman who took her time getting the message to you that the man convicted of killing our parents was innocent? Who is she?"

"Who are *you?*" Caroline asked.

He shook his head, his phone clasped in his hand as he backed from the room.

His sister stopped him. "You told me who I really am," she reminded him. "Don't you think it's fair that we find out who you really are?"

Thad shook his head and groaned. "I can't."

"Our son is missing," Caroline said. "Maybe his kidnapping has to do with your parents' killer and maybe it has to do with whatever you're keeping from us."

"We can't help you unless we know everything," Detective Kendall said. "We might be wasting our time chasing down the wrong leads."

"I'll find that out after I make a couple of calls," Thad promised.

"To whom?" Caroline demanded to know. "Who are you calling?"

He closed his eyes, as if praying for divine intervention. Then finally he answered them all, "My superior in the State Department."

Natalie's fiancé nodded as if he had confirmation of something he'd already learned. And he wrapped his arms around Natalie, offering her the comfort Caroline had refused to accept from Thad.

She'd only wanted the truth. But now that she knew…her mind reeled from all the possibilities. "You work for the government?" she asked.

Thad nodded.

"And you've been doing this for years?"

"I was recruited out of college," he admitted, holding her gaze while his family reacted with gasps of surprise.

She suspected that was another lie. He hadn't been *recruited;* he had sought them out, offering up his life for his country.

Or for excitement.

Or for justice.…

"So have you made a lot of enemies over the years?" She had to know.

"Only if my cover was blown," he said. "And until recently I was certain that it had never been compromised. You all just became some of a very small group of people who know that I'm more than a photojournalist."

"What happened recently?" Ash asked, ever the detective.

"When I left midassignment to come back here, one of my associates was abducted," Thad said, his blue eyes darkening with regret and guilt. "Before he was murdered, he was tortured."

Could that be happening now to their son? Could someone be torturing him?

She gasped in horror, and her legs gave out, folding beneath her.

THAD WAS TOO FAR AWAY to catch Caroline before she hit the floor. She never lost consciousness, though, or her anger and resentment at him. When he reached out to help her up, she shrank back from him, as if unable to bear his touch, and got to her feet herself.

"I wish you never came back," she whispered at him.

He didn't blame her for hating him. At the moment he hated himself for putting their son in danger.

"If he never came back, Gray and I would be dead," Natalie defended him.

He shook his head at his sister, not wanting anyone to further upset Caroline. His phone rang, with the call he'd been waiting to have returned, but he hesitated to reach for it. Not wanting to leave Caroline alone.

"Take it," she ordered him. "If it'll help you find my son, take the damn call."

He clicked the phone on. "Kendall…"

"Still no chatter," Anya replied without

greeting. "I don't believe you've been compromised."

"Someone stormed a day care center with a gun today and abducted my son," he told her, whether she cared or not.

She gasped. "I'm sorry."

"I don't need your sympathy. I need your help," he implored her. "I'm calling in every favor I've got coming. I need to find my son as soon as possible."

"I'll find out what I can from here," she promised, "and call back."

He clicked off the phone and turned to his family. "I want you all to do the same. Call in every favor you have coming."

Devin was already reaching for his phone, as was Gray and Ash. Aunt Angela reached for Caroline instead, wrapping her arm around her trembling body and offering her support.

"You need to lie down," his aunt told her, "and rest."

Caroline shook her head. "I can't…"

"You're going through the worst nightmare a parent can," she commiserated. "There's nothing anyone can do or say to comfort you. But you have to keep the faith that your son will come back to you. And when he does, you'll need to be strong."

Because the boy might be traumatized from what he'd seen.

Devin lifted his phone away from his ear. "Jolie pulled the old employee records from dead storage. She found Ed Turner's insurance applica—"

"Ed Turner?" Uncle Craig interrupted. "He hasn't worked at the company in decades. He quit long before your parents were murdered. He started up his own company. Hell, Devin, you've been trying to get your hands—"

"I didn't think it was him, either," Devin said. "But Aunt Angela put him on the list."

When her husband turned to her, Angela nodded. "I suspected back then…"

"But he was married, too. His wife just died."

"Not every man is as honorable as you are," Aunt Angela told her husband, her eyes warm with love for him.

"But what could Ed want with Thad's son?" Uncle Craig asked, his brow furrowed with confusion. "He has his own money."

"According to the records Jolie found," Devin said, "he also had a son named Wade with a date of birth making him about a year older than you, Thad."

Uncle Craig sucked in a breath as he realized what Thad had long ago. This wasn't about money or even the past. At least not the two decades-old past. It was about revenge.

"The dentist is listed," Devin said, "so she's getting Rachel the information to verify dental records."

Thad was glad that his brothers had been as clever as he was and had fallen for smart, resourceful women. He turned toward Ash. "You got an address for Turner yet?"

"Too many of them," Ash said with a sigh. "The guy and his corporation own properties all over St. Louis and the surrounding areas. We have to run them all down."

"We need to hurry," he said.

He wasn't sure how much time his son had, if he had any left at all.

CAROLINE WASN'T LIKE THAD'S brothers' wife and fiancée. She wasn't a crime-scene tech or even all that computer savvy. She didn't know how to chase down leads to her son's whereabouts. She didn't have the slightest idea how to find her son. But she knew he wasn't at the Kendall estate.

And she hadn't wanted to be there, either.

Her son had gotten away from his kidnapper at the mall. What if he'd escaped him again and found someone to drive him home? He knew his address. So she held her breath as she opened the door, hoping he waited for her inside and would rush into her arms.

But her house was eerily quiet and empty. No Mark. She wasn't alone, though. Thad had insisted on driving her home.

No matter what she said to him or how coldly she treated him, he had been considerate and patient with her. Of course he was used to kidnappings and to violence. She hadn't been until his world had collided with hers.

"Aunt Angela was right," he said. Sliding his arm around her waist, he led her toward the stairs. "You should get some rest."

"How?" Her heart pounded erratically, and her legs shook.

He supported most of her weight up the stairs and down the short hall to her room.

"Do you have anything you can take that will help you sleep?" he asked, his blue eyes dark with concern for her as she dropped onto the edge of her bed.

She wasn't the one he needed to worry about; he needed to worry about their child.

"My son," she said. "I need Mark back in my arms. I won't sleep until he's home." Her voice cracked as emotion welled up inside her. "I want my son."

But her baby was gone....

"I'll bring him home to you," Thad promised.

"You don't even know for sure who has him," she reminded him. Sure, Ed Turner sounded like the most viable suspect, but because of Thad, there were so many. "You have so many enemies."

"I'm sorry."

She shook her head. "I know it's not your fault. You were just doing your job. You didn't even know about Mark." She sucked in a breath. "So I blame myself."

He dropped to his knees in front of her, as if begging her forgiveness. "None of this was your fault," he said. "I should have stayed away. I had no right to try to be part of your lives, not with the life I've lived."

"You're a hero," she reminded him. "You saved your sister's life and her fiancé's. And you've probably saved countless other lives."

"There's only one life I'm worried about right now."

Their son's.

He cupped her face in his hands, so that their gazes met and held. "I will find him."

But would it be too late?

"Then go," she urged. He shouldn't be wasting his time with her. "Do whatever you have to do to track down the man who took our son."

"I don't want to leave you alone," he said.

"Mark needs you more than I do," she reminded him. He had skills that no one else in the St. Louis Police Department possessed, not even his brother.

He nodded and reached beneath his jacket and pulled out a gun. "I'm leaving you this."

She shuddered. "I don't want that."

"I won't leave you alone unless you keep it," he said.

She shook her head. "But I don't like guns."

"When we dated, I took you to the shooting range," he said, reminding her of the date she'd found so exciting and so unlike her usual routine.

"That was my first clue that you were more than just a photojournalist," she said. He'd been an expert shot and very familiar with the weapons.

"You were a natural," he said. "Do you remember what I showed you about how to take off the safety and aim?"

She nodded. She hadn't forgotten anything he'd taught her, but she still hesitated before reaching for it. "I really don't want to have a gun in the house with a child."

But the child wasn't there. And if Thad didn't leave to find him, Mark might never come home. So she grabbed the gun and immediately tucked it into the drawer of the bedside table.

"He'll be home again," Thad said as if he'd read her mind. "I'll bring him home to you."

Thad had never made her promises, not four years ago and not since he'd been back… until today. She didn't know if that meant he would be able to keep his promise, but at least she knew that he would try, that he would probably die trying.

She leaned forward and pressed a kiss to his lips. His breath shuddered out against her mouth, and he kissed her back.

She pulled back when she tasted tears. They were hers. She'd cried so many she was numb to them. But she brushed the moisture from his face and mouth and implored, "Be careful...."

She didn't want to lose them both, but a shiver raced down her spine with foreboding. And she knew their Christmas was going to be far from merry.

Chapter Thirteen

His heart thudding in his chest, Thad studied the blowup of Ed Turner's DMV photo and compared it to the police artist sketch of the man who'd taken Mark. "It's definitely him."

"It's the guy the day care director described hanging around earlier. I should have called you about him, but he'd gone into the coffee shop, so they'd figured he'd just been waiting to meet someone." Ash, sitting in the driver's seat of the unmarked St. Louis PD cruiser, studied the house across the street from where he'd parked.

This neighborhood wasn't as nice or well kept as Caroline's. The houses were smaller, older, in various states of disrepair or totally abandoned. It was hard to tell which of the last two was Turner's house.

Was he there just living in squalor, or had he abandoned it all together?

"This doesn't make any sense," Ash said, shaking his head in confusion. "Of all the properties he owns—the high-rise condos or that three-story mansion near the country club, why would he be staying at this dump?"

"This was Wade Turner's last known address," Thad reminded him. "And Wade Turner was the man I killed, right?"

"His dental records match those of the man you killed," Ash confirmed.

That was why Ed Turner had gone off the grid—he'd been grieving. "You said he's owned this house for a while."

"Property records show that he and his wife bought it when they were first married thirty-five years ago," Ash said with a glance at his laptop, which was balanced between his seat and Thad's. "Ed kept it even after they moved up. His son had been living in it for the past several years. Wade never really held down a job. With his mother slipping him his father's money, he hadn't needed one. He lived here for free and got enough money for drugs and alcohol."

"He had a problem with both?"

"Not enough to get him arrested, but enough for him to turn up as a person of interest from time to time."

"Until he turned up in the morgue."

"Ed never claimed his body. Are you sure he even noticed he was missing?" Ash wondered. "It sounds like they were estranged for a while."

"Wade was still his son," Thad said. "Ed would have recognized that picture from the ATM footage."

"It was grainy and hard to see—"

"Wade was his son, and I killed him," Thad said. "And that's why Ed Turner abducted my son. He wants an eye for an eye."

Which meant that Mark might already be dead. Thad reached for the door handle. He couldn't wait for the Special Response Team that Ash had called in. He had to know now if his son was alive or dead.

His brother's hand grasped his shoulder. "You're not going anywhere."

"I'm going to bring my son home." He'd promised Caroline.

The fear and pain on her beautiful face haunted him. Her image had been burned on his mind for the past four years. But always when he'd thought about her, she had been smiling and happy. Not devastated like she was now.

"If Turner really is as dangerous as you

think, you're going to get yourself killed," Ash said.

"You may want to wait for backup," Thad said, "but I don't need it."

On most of his assignments, he hadn't had it, and those assignments had usually gone smoother than when he'd had help.

"Even when backup gets here, you can't go in there with us," Ash said, acting more like a protective big brother than a detective.

"The hell I—"

"You're not authorized."

"One phone call and I'll be leading this investigation," Thad warned him. "I have more authority than you do. Hell, I have more authority than the whole St. Louis PD."

"More ego, too," Ash retorted.

"More at stake," Thad corrected him.

"Exactly," his brother agreed. "You're too involved."

"He's my son." And that may have already cost the little boy his life.

Ash glanced back where the SRT van was pulling up along the street, out of the line of vision of the house they were watching. He blew out a ragged breath and then dragged in a deep one. "They're here."

Thad wasn't so sure that was a good thing,

a SWAT team storming the house. "Keep them back."

"Until I assess the situation," Ash said.

"I'll assess the situation." He had to get close enough to see inside, to see if his son lived.

Ash shook his head. "Let me do this for you. Stay out here."

Thad shook his head. "I can't do that." Even though his heart pounded erratically with fear over what they might find inside....

"Thad—"

"I've seen things," he reminded his brother. "You have no idea the things I've seen."

"I was over there, too." Ash reminded him of his deployment. "I've seen things. But if you're right about Turner, this—"

"Is wasting time." And he'd already done enough of that trying to convince everyone else that it didn't matter what facade Ed Turner showed the world: successful businessman, humanitarian, leader in lifesaving military communications—he was still a killer. He had brutally murdered two people in their beds twenty years ago. He had killed Thad's parents; he probably wouldn't hesitate to kill his son, too.

"Let's go." Shaking off Ash's hand on his

arm, he threw open the door and, keeping below the other cars parked on the street, he headed toward the house.

Ash stayed close behind him, covering his back and keeping as low as Thad did. The only sound he made was the command he whispered into the radio pinned to his shirt collar. "Stand down until I give the order."

Ash wouldn't be giving the order. Thad didn't need backup, not even his brother. All he needed was his son. He crept close to the house. The paint, which might have once been white, was now gray and peeling off the weathered wood. Icicles hung low from the eaves, dripping despite the cold temperatures, probably because there was no insulation in the attic. Or the walls.

If Mark was inside, he would be cold. And scared.

Thad rose just high enough to peer through a window. But newspapers had been taped over the glass. He couldn't see inside, not even a shadow or a flash of light. Maybe that was good, though, because then Turner couldn't see out, either.

"We need SRT," Ash said. "They have infrared and heat sensors. They can tell us if there's anyone inside."

The heat sensor only worked if the person was alive. So it wouldn't tell Thad everything he needed to know. He would only learn that with his own eyes. He walked away from the house, causing his brother to gasp and stare at in him surprise.

Thad needed that element of surprise. So after he'd walked a few strides away, he turned back and ran, hurling himself through that newspaper-covered window. Glass shattered and caught at his clothes and skin. He didn't feel any pain; he was totally focused on the room.

He swung his barrel toward the doorways, expecting Turner to rush inside with his gun barrel pressed to Mark's temple—if the child was still alive. But nothing moved inside the house. Not a creak or a curse. Then someone breathed—and it wasn't Thad. He was still holding his breath. The breath turned to a gasp and then a cry.

"Daddy!"

A little boy shifted out of the corner of the couch where he'd been cowering. He vaulted at Thad, throwing his arms around his neck.

Thad clasped him close with one arm while he kept his gun raised. More cautiously, Ash stepped through the window.

"Thank God," he murmured when he saw father and son.

"Where's the man?" Thad asked, not wanting his brother to step into a trap as he moved around, securing the house.

"My new friend, Ed?"

Bile rose in Thad's throat, but he nodded. "Where is Ed?"

A smile of anticipation curved Mark's little bow-shaped mouth. "He went to get Mommy for me."

"What?"

"He's going to bring her here, so me and her can be together," Mark explained. "Ed told me that you would come later, but you'd be late…like you were that day at the mall."

Turner had meant Thad would be too late—too late to save his family. He hugged the little boy tight, like he should have held Caroline.

He shouldn't have left her alone even with the gun. Caroline was too softhearted to use it, even to save herself.

Thad had known that, but he'd still left her alone, thinking she would be safer at her house than out looking for their son with him. His only hope was that the police cars patrolling her neighborhood stopped Ed before he broke into her home. He couldn't lose Caroline.

THE BLAST AND TINKLE of shattering glass snapped Caroline out of her daze of fear and concern for her son's safety. Still clutching his teddy bear, she jumped up from where she'd been sitting on Mark's bed, rushed toward the stairs and peered over the railing.

A man rolled across her living-room floor, toppling the Christmas tree before regaining his feet. He was an older man, probably nearly as old as Thad's uncle Craig. Like Craig Kendall, he was also very good-looking with blond hair and dark eyes. But beneath the handsome facade was a madness and rage that had a sense of foreboding racing across Caroline's skin.

He must have been the man she'd felt watching her and Mark. Was he the one who'd grabbed her son? She wanted to confront him, to yell at him and demand he tell her where Mark was.

But Mark wasn't with him. Did that mean her son had gotten away? Had Thad rescued him?

Because if the man had Mark, why would he have come for her? To kill her?

She swallowed a squeak of fear, but he must have heard her.

A gun clutched in his hand, he whirled toward the stairwell. And her. She grabbed a lamp from the hall table and hurled it down at him. The porcelain struck his shoulders, eliciting an oath from him as it cracked and broke.

He fired the gun, embedding the bullet in the wall behind her head. She screamed and ran for her bedroom. And the gun Thad had left her.

But could she use it?

She slammed her door and turned the lock, which was probably too flimsy to keep out anyone. So she rushed toward her dresser and pushed the heavy oak piece of furniture toward the door, which was already rattling under a pounding fist.

Then, sitting on the floor, she used just her legs and shoved the dresser against the door. But since she could move it, so could he. It wouldn't even take him as long or as much effort.

Her hand shaking, she reached for the bed-side table and pulled out the gun. Because she was shaking so badly, she fumbled with the safety before getting it off.

But would she be able to get off a shot before he got her? The doorjamb splintered as the lock broke the wood. And then the door slammed into the back of the dresser.

Again and again, like an axe swinging at a log.

The piece of furniture rocked back and forth before finally, slowly, falling forward. The mirror struck the floor and shattered, sending a shower of glass flying at Caroline like confetti on New Year's Eve.

She doubted she would see New Year's, though, or even Christmas.

Unless she fired first.

So she raised the barrel of the gun toward the door and pressed her finger against the trigger.

Chapter Fourteen

Each shot sent a bullet of fear through Thad's heart. He vaulted through the shattered picture window and staggered across the floor, stumbling over the fallen Christmas tree. Regaining his balance on all the broken glass and ornaments, he ran across the living room and up the steps to the second story.

To Caroline.

The trim around her bedroom door had splintered. Some pieces of wood lay on the floor in the hall while others had been pushed inside with the door. Fearful of what he might find—like at Turner's house—Thad edged closer to the opening.

But it wasn't open—not entirely. A turned-over dresser blocked half the doorway. Thad leaned in just as a bullet whizzed past his head and struck the wall behind him. He lifted his gun to fire back but, as he zeroed in on the shooter, he lowered the barrel. "Caroline!"

"Oh, my God!" she shrieked as she dropped her gun. "Did I shoot you? Are you all right?"

She climbed over the back of the dresser, reaching for him. He knelt on the wood and clasped her tight in his arms.

"Are you all right?" he asked, pulling back to stare at her face. Nicks and cuts marred the silky perfection of her skin. "You're hurt."

She shook her head. "It was the glass from the mirror."

The mirror of the dresser she'd been strong and smart enough to push across the door, to buy herself some time to retrieve the gun.

He couldn't have been more proud of her.

"Is he gone?" she asked. "Did I shoot him?"

"He's not dead," he said, almost regretful that he'd found no body lying in the hall.

But Turner may have still been inside the house. Thad had left Ash outside, to guard what else mattered most to him.

He grabbed up his weapon again. "Stay here. I'm going to finish searching the house and then go back outside."

She reached out, clutching at him. "Don't leave me."

She wasn't talking about just physically.

She didn't want Turner attacking him as he had her.

"I'll be right back," he promised her.

Unless Ed Turner waited somewhere in the house, ready to ambush him.

HOW LONG HAD HE BEEN GONE?

She hadn't heard any more shots, but she hadn't heard anything else, either. Just the eerie silence that had reigned before the glass shattered.

She lifted her head, straining for a noise, any noise. And finally, she heard footfalls on the steps. Someone was coming back upstairs. She grabbed the gun again.

But she couldn't fire it and risk almost hitting the wrong person. Almost hitting someone she loved. Instead, she tucked the weapon back inside the drawer of the bedside table.

She was just heading toward the bathroom to lock herself inside there when she heard a soft voice. "What happened to the Christmas tree? Will Santa still be able to put presents under it?"

Thad carried their boy down the hall toward her. She ran to greet them, pulling Mark into her arms to squeeze his warm little body tight.

Her voice shaking with tears, she asked, "Are you all right, sweetheart?"

"I missed you, Mommy," he said, winding his arms around her neck. "My new friend, Ed, was going to come get you for me."

She shivered and not just because cold winter air blew through her broken picture window. "That man is not your friend, honey," she corrected him. "He's a stranger."

"Ed told me that he's Aunt Natalie's dad," Mark said, "and that makes him family."

And all Mark had wanted for Christmas. Even the shopping mall Santa had been surprised that he hadn't asked for a toy or a video game.

Thad patted his son's back. "That man didn't tell you the truth."

The little boy's blue eyes widened with shock.

Maybe Caroline shouldn't have protected him so much from the realities of the world.

"Ed lied?" Mark asked.

Thad uttered a ragged sigh. "Aunt Natalie's dad and mine died a long time ago."

She waited, worried that he might tell the little boy more than he was ready to learn about the world. But he stopped himself and met her gaze over Mark's head.

"And I need to go catch the man responsible for his death," he continued. But he was talking to her now, not their son.

She nodded in complete understanding.

"I searched the whole house before I took Mark from Ash and brought him inside. Turner isn't here. But I want to take the two of you to the estate," he said. "To make sure you'll be safe."

She shook her head. "He's been through too much already."

"Exactly."

"It's getting late," she said. Afternoon had slipped into evening. Her son had been gone too long. "He'll sleep better in his own bed."

"But the window—"

"Can be repaired tonight." Being a single mom and home owner, she'd made certain to find a trusty handyman long ago.

"But what about security?"

"Is the estate any more secure?" she asked. "It's been broken into, too." Twice. But she didn't need to remind him of that.

He sighed again. "You're right. There's only one way to guarantee the security of the people I love." He leaned forward and pressed a kiss to Mark's forehead. Despite the excitement he'd had that day, the little boy's eyes were already drifting closed.

Then Thad kissed her, too, brushing his lips across hers. None of the danger she and her son had gone through was really his fault, yet she held on to her resentment against him. It was the only way to protect her heart from breaking when he intended to put himself in danger to apprehend their son's kidnapper.

When he pulled back, hurt flashed in his eyes that she hadn't responded to his kiss. "I'm sorry," he said, "about everything. I don't blame you for being mad at me. I'm mad at myself. I thought for sure that I shook whoever might have followed me, but instead I led him right here—" his chest rose with an agitated breath "—to you and Mark."

She opened her mouth, ready to absolve him. But before she could, he continued, "I'll do what I should have the day after Mark was grabbed at the mall. I'll make sure the St. Louis PD has a unit in the driveway until Turner's caught."

"Done," Ash assured them as he climbed the stairs. "And we'll get someone here to fix your window."

"Thank you," she said to Detective Kendall. But her gratitude was for Thad because he'd brought her son home just as he had promised.

Now if only she could get him to promise to bring himself safely home to her.

But this man, Turner, may have gotten away with murder twenty years ago, if he was the one responsible for Thad's parents' deaths. So she knew Thad would not rest until the man had finally been brought to justice.

Her arms aching with the weight of her soundly sleeping son, she turned for his bedroom. The brothers talked behind her.

"We have units sitting on Turner's house, too," Ash said. "In case he goes back, thinking the boy's still there."

"This guy is good," Thad said. "He's been looking over his shoulder for twenty years, worried that his past would finally catch up with him. He's not going to walk into a trap. I suspect that he even got training…where I got training, when he was setting up those defense contracts."

"I don't care how damn good he is. He won't get away again," Ash said, his voice gruff with anger.

"No, he won't," Thad said. "He doesn't intend to."

"What do you mean?"

"I'll meet you downstairs," Thad said, dismissing his brother to follow Caroline into Mark's room. "I can't believe he's out."

Thad pulled back the blankets for her to lay Mark onto his bed. She slipped off his boots and pulled the blankets back up to his chin, which was damp from the drool trailing out of the corner of his open mouth.

"Kids are resilient," she assured him. She'd seen some of her students bounce back from tragedies. "And thankfully he's too young to really understand what happened."

In case they were going to discuss what happened, she walked from her son's room and, when Thad followed her into the hall, pulled his door shut. She hated losing sight of him for even that minute, but Thad had thoroughly checked the house before bringing their son inside. So the bogeyman wasn't waiting in his closet, ready to grab him the minute she stepped away.

If only she really believed that.

She needed to get rid of the other danger to her son now. So she walked the short distance down the hall to her room, stepped over her dresser and retrieved the gun from her bedside table. Careful not to point it at him again, she extended the handle toward Thad.

Instead of taking it, he busied himself with righting her dresser and pushing it back where it had been.

"The department people need to clean up the glass in here," he remarked. "Or you're going to get hurt."

It was too late for that.

"I'm more worried about me or Mark getting hurt if I keep this gun in the house," she said, hating the weight and coldness of the weapon in her hand.

"But if you insist on staying here, you'll need that for protection."

She shook her head.

"You must have scared off Turner with it," he pointed out.

"But I nearly shot you."

"It's not like I didn't have it coming," he said with a halfhearted grin.

"Just take it," she urged him. "I don't want it in the house with Mark." She'd heard too many stories about what happened when guns were left around curious children.

"I didn't scare him...with what I told him about Turner?" Thad asked as he finally grabbed the handle of the gun.

She shook her head. "He needs to know the man is not his friend."

Because she understood what Thad's brother did not—Ed Turner was not done with them. Maybe she should have kept the gun.

But the thought of Mark getting a hold of it...

She shuddered. She had nearly lost him once, and she wouldn't survive if something happened to her son. Or Thad.

She stared at him, committing his every handsome feature to memory. She worried that when he left her this time, he would never be coming back.

Thad met her gaze, as if he were ready to flinch at what he'd see there. "I don't blame you for hating me. I hate myself for putting you two in danger."

Tears burned her eyes, so she shut them to clear away the sting. And when she opened them, Thad was gone. He wouldn't hear her words, but she uttered them anyway. "I don't hate you."

She just loved him too much to lose him again.

TURNER WASN'T SURPRISED to find police cars parked along his street. They were unmarked, but by just being late models, they stuck out like sore thumbs among the rust buckets parked in front of the run-down houses. He should have maintained the house better. Simply keeping it hadn't been enough to honor Emily.

But that was all he'd ever done. Kept her but never really taken care of her. It wasn't surprising that when she'd finally gone to the doctor, she had been sick too long for treatment. He'd loved her. But, just like this house, he'd ignored her.

Because she hadn't been as pretty or charming or vivacious as Marie Kendall. And he had been a bewitched fool instead of a man.

Joseph and Marie had been so rich and beautiful and powerful. They had reminded him of the characters Tom and Daisy from *The Great Gatsby*. And just like Tom and Daisy, they had been careless people. Joseph hadn't cared whom he'd used to build his company, destroying other businesses to build his. And Marie hadn't cared whom she'd hurt in her endless quest for attention. She'd destroyed marriages and families and neglected her own children.

He recited aloud a quote from the book.

"They were careless people, Tom and Daisy—they smashed up things and creatures and then retreated back into their money or their vast carelessness, or whatever it was that kept them together, and let other people clean up the mess they had made." Twenty years ago, Ed had cleaned up their mess when he'd killed them, and he'd saved their children and future victims from their vast carelessness.

And how had Thad Kendall repaid him? By killing his son.

"Wade…"

Poor Wade. The kid had never had a chance. He'd never had a father. Ed had been too obsessed with building his company, with trying to prove to Marie Kendall that he could be every bit as rich and successful as Joseph.

He could have never built his company big enough or his houses opulent enough to impress Marie, though. Or for her to let him claim his daughter.…

Emily hadn't cared about the money Ed had made or all the houses Ed had built. She had always loved this first one best. She had always loved Ed best.

Maybe that was why, of all the condos and homes Wade could have lived in, he had chosen his mother's favorite house. He had been a good son to his mother. And in the end, he had been a good son to Ed even though Ed had never given his son what he'd deserved from his father.

He'd never given him love or attention.

Now it was too late. But Ed had made him a promise. Justice. He had promised to avenge his death, and this time Ed would not fail his son. He'd gotten away with murder before. He probably wouldn't this time, but he didn't care anymore. He had nothing left to care about, and soon, neither would Thad Kendall.

Chapter Fifteen

Thad had commandeered the St. Louis PD interrogation room for his personal interviews. He'd talked to everyone he'd been able to round up who'd ever known or spoken to or just passed Ed Turner on the damn street.

Ruthless businessman.

Generous philanthropist.

Inventive genius.

Loving husband.

Supportive father.

Those were the statements he hadn't bothered to write down, having already committed them to memory. Along with every other thing he had learned about Ed Turner in the past twelve hours. But those statements were superficial, from people who'd really never known Ed Turner at all.

Just as so many people had really never

known Thad Kendall. Except for Caroline. She knew him.

And Ed's recently deceased, long-suffering wife of thirty-five years had known Turner best. Thad hadn't been able to bring her into the interrogation room. But he'd found the next best thing in the house where Mark had been held.

Her diaries. She had recorded all her hopes and fears. She'd known everything about her husband, even why he was an alcoholic.

"We've got all his usual bars and liquor stores staked out," Ash said, pressing his fist over his mouth to stanch a yawn. He had been awake all night, too, at Thad's side for every interview, probably because he hadn't trusted his younger brother to conduct them without resorting to torture.

But in the end it had come down to what they'd read, not what they'd heard. Ash tapped the cover of the journal he'd just finished. "Eventually he'll run out of whatever liquor he had with him," Ash said, "and he'll go for more."

Thad shook his head. His gut told him that Ed Turner had quit drinking...the day Thad shot and killed his son. Otherwise he wouldn't have been clearheaded enough to follow a spy without being detected and to figure out what mattered most to Thad.

His heart clutched at the image he'd burned into his mind—Mark with his arms wound tight around his mother's neck and Caroline clinging to the baby she'd thought lost to her forever.

Because of Thad.

He really wouldn't blame her if she hated him. He hated himself for putting them in danger. "You're sure they're safe?"

As he had every other time Thad had asked him, Ash assured him, "I have my best men sitting on her house. They won't let Turner get to your son or your..." He peered up at Thad, who was too agitated to sit down. "What is Caroline to you? Just the mother of your child?"

"What is Rachel to you?"

"The love of my life," Ash answered automatically and from his heart.

Thad rubbed his hands over his face, which was rough with stubble. "That's what Caroline is to me. It's what she was four years ago."

"But you never brought her around. You never mentioned her."

"I knew I had to leave her." And introducing her to the family, and knowing how she would have instantly become a part of it, would have made it impossible for him to do that. "It was the hardest thing I've ever had to do."

"But you're planning on doing it again," Ash reminded him. "You're planning on leaving her and your son."

"I have no choice."

"You have a choice. Hell, you're a Kendall. You have a lot of choices. You could work anywhere in St. Louis—local television stations. Hell, national stations. At Kendall Communications. Or even here," Ash said, his voice deep with emotion, "with me."

Thad smiled, moved that his brother would make such an offer. "I thought I had too much ego for you to want to work with me."

"I could beat it out of you," Ash replied with a quick and cocky grin, "just like I did when we were kids."

Thad was surprised to find a grin on his own lips. "Why do I have a feeling that we'd both be visiting Uncle Craig's office a lot if we worked together?"

Ash shuddered. "You were never *summoned* as often as Devin and I were. Don't understand why Dev wanted to work there."

"I do," Thad admitted.

Ash laughed.

"No. I'm serious."

"Why? Because Dad built the company?"

Having been only eleven when Joseph Kendall had been murdered, Thad hadn't idolized his father like his brothers had. He'd idolized Uncle Craig instead. "Because some of those advances our family company has made in communications have saved lives."

"You're talking spy techie stuff."

Thad nodded. "And military. We could use some of that kind of equipment now to track down Ed Turner. Hell, we need *his* stuff to do that. His is better, and that's why we keep losing contracts to him."

Ash chuckled. "You're usually half a world away, but you keep up on the family business better than I do and I live down the street from the office."

"I'm more concerned about where Turner is right now." They'd found where he'd been staying last; they had units going past his other properties. Where the hell was he?

Frustration gnawed at him. He would not be able to sleep or eat or even rest until Ed Turner was at the very least behind bars, at the most six feet under with his stalker son.

"You don't need the special equipment," Ash said. "Your interviews got us everything we need to know to track down Ed Turner. We really could use you in the department, even if you just gave classes on interrogation techniques."

"You wouldn't let me use all the techniques I know," Thad reminded him.

"You didn't need them." Ash laughed. "Maybe you do suck because we actually just needed Emily Turner's diaries. From reading those, I know where we'll find Ed Turner."

Thad shook his head, unconvinced that Turner was still drinking. Something as traumatic as losing a son could cause a sober man to drink. And it could cause a drunk to sober up.

"Don't you remember what she'd written?" Ash asked. "About how, if Ed was actually in town, he would ruin the boy's holiday because he'd tie on the drunk of all drunks on Christmas Eve." He glanced at his watch. "It's Christmas Eve now."

Christmas Eve.

"I know where Turner is," he said. "And he's not at a bar or liquor store."

Ash tensed. "The estate? I put a patrol

there, too, just in case he returned to the scene again."

No, Turner intended to create a new scene. For Thad.

CAROLINE SLEPT ON THE EDGE of Mark's single-size mattress, her arms wrapped tight around her son. Or she tried to sleep.

She was caught somewhere in that point between light sleep and being fully awake. Probably because Mark was restless, his elbows and feet jabbing into her as he moved in his sleep.

Kids were resilient. But her little man had been through an awful lot that he wasn't mature enough to process.

She would talk to the school psychologist about having Mark meet with a professional or giving Caroline the tools to help her son herself. After what had happened, she was unlikely to let Mark out of her sight for a while.

Now a shiver chased down her spine and not just because Mark had stolen all the blankets but because she had that odd sensation of being watched. The police officers were outside, parked in her driveway as she'd learned from his brother that Thad had been every night since Mark had nearly been abducted from the mall.

That was probably why Ed Turner had decided to take Mark from the day care. He'd known then that it would be easier than getting past Thad, who would die for his son.

And for her…

Had he? Was that why she had that odd feeling?

Then suddenly she knew why—because a cold barrel was pressed against her temple.

"Don't scream," a man advised her. "Don't even move."

Despite his warning, she moved slightly, trying to cover Mark with her body.

"Where's that gun?" he asked, pressing the barrel harder against her temple.

She swallowed hard, choking down her nerves and fear. "I—I gave it back to Thad."

Her voice, or Turner's, awakened Mark, who murmured then rubbed at his eyes.

"Shh…" She soothed her son. "Go back to sleep."

"It's nearly morning," Turner said, gesturing toward where light snuck around the edges of the shade on Mark's window. "And he must know what today is. After all, he is a Kendall."

She would have shaken her head but his gun held it still. "He's an Emerson, not a Kendall."

Turner laughed. "I don't care what his last name is. The kid is definitely a Kendall and definitely Thad Kendall's son."

"Hurting him won't bring your son back, Mr. Turner," she said.

"Thad made sure my boy could never come back," he said, his voice gruff with bitterness and anguish. The man might have been a killer, but he'd also been a father. And that father was grieving.

"Thad was only protecting his family," she reminded him. "Your son was trying to kill his sister."

Ed shook his head. "Wade figured everything out, you know. He finally understood why I'd done everything I had." He expelled a shaky sigh. "Why I'd failed him and his mother so much…"

"He loved you," she said, grasping at straws. She needed to keep him talking, needed to distract him so she could figure out how to save Mark. "He was trying to protect you from being arrested."

Ed sighed. "Yes, he was a good boy."

"I'm a good boy," Mark murmured sleepily.

"You are," Turner agreed. "It's just too bad…"

"You don't have to do this," Caroline said. "Please, don't do this."

"My daddy says you're not my friend," Mark said as he fully awakened and noticed the man standing over his bed, holding a gun on his mother. "And you're not just playing."

"No," Turner admitted almost regretfully. "I'm not just playing."

And no matter what Caroline said, she doubted he would change his mind from carrying out his revenge on Thad. He wanted Thad to suffer as much as he was suffering.

She regretted now not telling Thad earlier about Mark. He had missed all the important milestones the boy had already passed. He had missed so much, and now he would never have the chance to make up for what he'd missed.

And she would never have the chance to tell him how much she had loved him and would always love him…even after she was gone.

BLOOD COVERED THEIR FACES.

No matter how much carnage he'd seen in war, Thad knew he would never forget this sight—never get out of his mind finding bloodied bodies on Christmas Eve.

His hand shook as he reached out to check for a pulse. The skin was already cold, as cold as the blood now running through Thad's veins.

He lifted his cell phone to his mouth. It was on, his connection open to Ash, who'd been driving too slow and carefully. So Thad had lost him. "I'm sorry. Your guys are dead."

The police officers were slumped inside their car, one lying over the dash, the other over the steering wheel. Turner was definitely not drinking, not when he was able to move as quickly and dangerously as he had. He had definitely done more than just sell his equipment to soldiers and spies; he'd demonstrated how to use it himself.

He was exactly like Thad, more dangerous than he seemed.

Ash's curse crackled in the phone. "Wait for me and SRT."

"No."

"We're only a couple minutes out—"

"That'll be too late."

If it wasn't already....

If the same scene didn't await Thad inside the house.

"Don't you dare go in there," Ash said, his voice sharp with anger and fear. "It's a trap."

"I know."

And if Mark and Caroline were already gone, he didn't particularly care.

Chapter Sixteen

The policemen were dead. If they weren't, they would have tried to rescue her and Mark. But Caroline and Mark had been alone with the gunman, the killer, for a while now.

She hadn't been able to keep him talking. They had all fallen silent some time ago, Mark nodding off to sleep again in her arms as she sat in the living room next to the fallen Christmas tree.

But Ed Turner hadn't shot them yet. He was waiting.

For Thad.

"I'm a teacher," she said. "The most popular teacher at my elementary school." She wasn't bragging; she was trying to get him to know her, so that it wouldn't be as easy for him to shoot her as it had been for him to shoot the policemen who'd been guarding her and Mark. "My kids keep coming back to visit me. They threw me a baby shower when I was pregnant with Mark. I was alone when I had him, and I raised him alone for the first three years of his life. He means everything to me."

"And you mean everything to him," Turner assured her with an almost sympathetic smile. "When he was at my house, he talked about his daddy, but he wanted to be with his mommy."

Tears stung her eyes and tickled her nose. But she couldn't give in to them and risk succumbing to hysteria. He would probably shoot her then just to keep her quiet. And she would leave her son at the mercy of the madman.

"He was a good boy at your house," she said with all the certainty as if she had been there, too. "He always minds his manners and is considerate of other people."

"He was very good," Turner admitted. "He said *please* and *thank you* and even *may* instead of *can*. He's a smart kid."

"Very smart," she said with more than maternal pride—with an educator's assessment. "My second-graders aren't as polite and mature as Mark. He'll grow up to be a fine young man."

Turner's sympathy turned to pity now. And he shook his head. "No, he won't. But the two of you will be together, just like you both wanted."

She tried to suppress it, but a cry of dismay slipped through her lips. Mark shifted in her arms, reacting to the noise and her fear.

"I won't make you suffer," Turner promised.

"No, you just want to make me suffer," Thad remarked as he passed through the archway between the kitchen and living room.

She hadn't seen him. But Turner must have, because he stood far enough behind the foyer wall that Thad would not have been able to shoot him. Turner would have been able to shoot her and Mark, though.

"We've been waiting for you," Turner said with an edge of frustration. "You took your damn sweet time getting here."

"Sorry about that," Thad said conversationally, as if he was used to guns and violence and death.

But then Caroline reminded herself that he *was* used to all those things.

"Were you waiting for your brother and SWAT to back you up again?" Ed asked.

"They won't get in here fast enough to save them."

"Or you," Thad agreed. "But that's your plan, too."

"What?" His dark eyes narrowed as if he mentally tried to assess how much of his plan Thad had figured out.

"You want to kill yourself," Thad clarified.

Turner grinned and shook his head. "No, I want you to do it."

Thad nodded. "Death by cop."

"You're not a cop."

"No," he agreed. "But I'm not a reporter, either."

"Spy?"

Thad nodded. "I became one because of you."

That startled Turner enough to turn more fully toward Thad and away from her and Mark. She understood now what Thad was trying to do, distract Turner enough for her and Mark to get out of the line of fire.

While he stepped into it…while he gave up his life for hers.

She wanted to tell him now what she should have earlier. She didn't hate him at all. She loved him. But if he was successful, she would never get the chance.

Mark would never get to really know his father, either. But, as the little boy was awake now, and frozen with fear, he would forever remember the image of his father dying right in front of him.

He was too young now to understand the sacrifice his father was willing to make. He would only remember that Santa hadn't brought him what he'd wanted for Christmas this year. Instead he'd taken away the only chance of the boy ever having a family.

WHILE TURNER WAS FOCUSED ON HIM, Thad was focused on everything else. Ash and the SRT had arrived outside and were creeping toward the house. But they wouldn't burst inside until Ash heard the go word through the open cell connection.

And he wouldn't get the go word until Caroline and Mark were able to take some kind of cover. The fallen Christmas tree wouldn't protect them. But if Caroline could somehow flip over the couch and get herself and Mark behind it...

She wouldn't meet his gaze for him to try to convey the message to her. Was she still so angry with him that she couldn't stand to look at him? But then she was more focused on their son than on him. She had wrapped her arms tight around Mark, as if to shield his body. And she'd also covered his eyes and ears as if to shield his mind.

Turner laughed. "You're smooth, Kendall. I'll give you that, but you're not smart enough to fool me. Do you think I'd actually believe I had any influence on *your* life?"

"You, more than anyone else, has," Thad replied. And he realized as he said it that he spoke the truth. "When you killed my parents, you destroyed my childhood."

"Your parents did that," Turner said. "They weren't who you must have made them out to be in your mind. You idolized memories tainted by the way the media portrayed them."

"The media did romanticize them," Thad said.

"So you have no idea what they were really like," Turner insisted, as if he was trying to justify killing them. "You were much better off with your aunt and uncle."

"Yes," Thad readily agreed. "Aunt Angela and Uncle Craig were wonderful guardians to us. But you'd already done your damage that Christmas Eve you murdered my parents in their beds."

"I did you a favor when I killed Joseph and Marie," Turner said almost desperately. "I protected you from *them*. They didn't care who they hurt," Turner said in defense of his actions. "They would have hurt you, your brothers and *Natalie*—my daughter."

Thad nodded. "Probably. But they never would have hurt us as much as you had."

"I never laid a hand on any of you. I just went into Natalie's room. But after what I'd done, after losing my temper with Joseph and Marie, I knew I could never tell her I was her father." He glanced down at his hand, as if still seeing their blood on it.

That was what he would have seen every time he'd tried to see Natalie.

"And no matter how much success I'd earned," he said, "the Kendalls would always have *more*."

"More?"

"More money. More influence. More stuff."

"None of that mattered to us," Thad insisted.

Turner uttered a bitter laugh. "Tell Wade that. Oh, you can't…because you killed him." He turned back toward Caroline and Mark.

"You think we cared anything about the

stuff?" Thad asked. "You ruined Christmas for us. You didn't just take away our parents. You took away hope and wonder and joy. For the past twenty years not one of us ever had a *merry* Christmas."

He had Turner's attention again. But he cared less about distracting him than about telling him everything that Thad had just suddenly realized himself. "You gave us nightmares. Natalie used to wake up nearly every night with them, screaming over the memories she was only able to suppress when she was awake. When she was asleep, the blond-haired bogeyman with the dark eyes—" how had no one ever realized that it was Ed Turner she'd seen that night in her room? "—would come back, and this time he would take Uncle Craig and Aunt Angela and me and Devin and Thad. He would take everything away from her."

"I—I left her there because I didn't want that," Ed said, as if he'd made a great sacrifice in not kidnapping his own daughter.

"You want to make me suffer now," Thad reminded him, "because I saved her from your son. I saved your daughter's life, and you want to take revenge on me for that?"

Turner gasped as Thad's words finally

penetrated his rage and madness to the brilliant mind of the man who'd invented top-secret communications for the State Department. "Oh, my God…"

"You would rather have sweet Natalie, who you had already made suffer for twenty years, lose what little happiness she had just managed to finally find in her life?"

"No," Turner sputtered, "I—I didn't want her to suffer."

Thad shook his head as disgust overwhelmed him. "I became a spy because I hadn't been able to save my parents that night, because I hadn't been able to protect my family from the utter devastation of *your* careless actions."

"No." Turner shook his head. "It wasn't about that. Your parents only cared about money and status. Your mother would have affairs just for attention, to make herself feel desirable and special and to make your father jealous. She never really had any intention of leaving him. Not because she loved him but because she loved being his wife. She loved the money and the prestige of being Mrs. Joseph Kendall. She just used me."

But he had obviously fallen deeply in love with Marie Kendall.

"She did use you," Thad brutally agreed. He had no defense for his mother's actions. "She didn't care about you at all. You were just a means to an end."

"I left Kendall Communications," Turner said, "and started my own company. I was going to prove to her that I could be a better man than your father. That I could be richer and more successful. But while I was gone building my company, Joseph built his even bigger. And I realized that no matter what I did, I would never be enough for Marie."

"No," Thad said. "But you were enough for Emily."

Turner met his gaze, and grief filled his dark eyes. "Emily…"

"We found her diaries in the house. She loved you. She knew everything. And she loved you." He didn't dare look away from Turner, but he wanted to glance at Caroline, to see if she could ever love him like Emily Turner had loved Ed.

Unconditionally. No matter the monster he'd been. No matter where he'd been.

"I realized that, too," Ed said. "I never deserved her. I came home that Christmas, and I wanted to start over with her and Wade. Emily had worked on some charity event—

it was *The Nutcracker* ballet. She and Wade and I attended."

"We were there." He remembered jerking at his tie and scuffing his shoes. And his mother being mad that he and his brothers weren't behaving like little gentlemen. She'd wanted everyone to think they were the perfect family. Why did they have to act like animals? Why couldn't they act the perfect little princess like Natalie?

"I know," Ed said gravely. "I saw all of you. I saw *Natalie.* And I knew she was mine. And your mother had never had the decency to tell me that I had a daughter."

Caroline choked on a small cry of alarm and guilt. But she wasn't at all like his mother. The situation was entirely different.

But Thad didn't dare try to reassure her with even a glance much less a word. For the moment Turner had forgotten all about her and Mark.

But to save them, Thad had to remind the man that they were there.

"So you were pissed off and you killed her," Thad said. "Because you were mad and probably drunk. And you wanted revenge. Just like now."

Turner shook his head, but he wasn't able to voice a denial.

"You're not threatening my family for justice," Thad insisted, "because justice was done when I killed your son and saved your daughter. Killing my son and the woman I love won't be justice. It'll just be murder."

He uttered a heavy sigh of pity. "And that makes you the most careless person of all. A vengeful killer."

PANIC QUICKENED TURNER'S PULSE as the guilt rushed back over him. After twenty years of living with the burden, he had finally fought it off only for Thad Kendall's words to settle the weight back onto his shoulders.

He wasn't that kind of man, or Emily wouldn't have loved him like she had for as long as she had.

He shook his head in denial. "You're wrong. It's not about revenge."

"It's not about justice, either," Kendall said. "Not unless you wanted your son to kill your daughter. Is that what you wanted?"

His stomach churned as the truth rose to the top. "No." To him she would always be the sweet little girl who'd looked like a princess that night at the ballet and an angel that night as she lay sleeping and he came to her room.

"I had to kill him," Kendall insisted. "It was the only way to save Natalie's life because he was determined to end it."

"That was my fault," Ed admitted. "I wasn't a real father to him. I was never around—I was off trying to build my company." Trying to be Joseph Kendall. "I left him and his mother alone so much. Then after she died and he found her diaries…"

His breath shuddered out as he remembered the final confrontation with his son. At the cemetery after everyone else had left, Wade had verbally and even physically assaulted him. Ed had let him get in the one blow, knowing he deserved it. But he'd stopped him and tried to hold him, had tried to apologize and explain…just as he'd been trying to explain to Thad. "He blamed me for breaking his mother's heart. Hell, I think he blamed me for her cancer." And maybe that had been Ed's fault. If he'd been home more, if he'd taken better care of her… Wade had been right to blame him. "He hated me."

"He wouldn't have tried to protect you had he really hated you," Kendall argued. "Despite everything, he loved you."

"I gave him no reason to love me," Ed said, the misery eating at him. His hand began to shake as finally he succumbed to the effects of alcohol withdrawal. He'd started drinking even before that Christmas Eve. He'd started drinking when Marie had refused his offer to leave Emily.

But he had control. He could handle it. Just a little shot in his coffee in the morning. A drink at lunch, just enough to take the edge of his anger and his regrets.

"How long has it been since you've had a drink?" Thad asked. Of course he would notice Ed's shakes; the guy didn't miss much.

If Ed hadn't stopped drinking, he never would have kept up let alone gotten the jump on Kendall. He'd known from that single kill shot that the man was more than just a photojournalist. Just as Ed had been more than a communications company owner. He was a killer, too.

"I haven't been drinking since that night they showed Wade's picture on the news," he admitted. "Even from that grainy security cam footage, I recognized my son. I knew it was him." Probably more because of the sick feeling in his gut than that horrible security still photo.

"He used to be a good kid," Ed defended his boy. "He was smart, too. I think he always knew I was guilty. He woke up that night I came home from killing your parents. He thought I was Santa Claus...until he saw the blood."

Kendall shuddered.

"Yours wasn't the only Christmas I ruined," Ed pointed out. Maybe because he hadn't been sober long enough, he hadn't realized before everything he'd taken from the Kendall children. Not just their parents, however sorry excuses they'd been for a mother and a father. He had taken away their childhoods, just as he had taken away Wade's.

"He was only eleven," Thad reminded him. "He would have been too young to figure out what happened. He didn't know then that Natalie was his sister, did he?"

"No," Ed replied. "I couldn't have told him that. And when that other man was arrested for the Christmas Eve Murders, I think he forgot all about that night."

"Until that man was cleared of the conviction."

He nodded. "That was around the same time his mother died, and he found her diaries. Then he put it all together and realized what I had done twenty years ago, that Natalie was mine."

"He hadn't wanted just to kill her, though," Thad said. "He had wanted to hide your guilt."

Ed groaned as the pain overwhelmed him. "No one could hide my guilt. I wasn't ever able to even drink it away. I can't go on like this. And I can't let my son die alone."

He lifted his gun. But he was too much a coward to pull the trigger himself. Or he would have committed suicide years ago. All he had to do was point his gun at Thad Kendall's family.

Even though Thad Kendall had already figured out Ed's plan, he wouldn't take the risk that Ed might actually shoot his son and the woman he loved. He put his finger on the trigger and waited, hoping Kendall wouldn't make him press it before he fired the first shot.

Chapter Seventeen

The gunshot echoed through the living room. Then the room exploded, bodies catapulting through windows and doors. Guns drawn and pointed.

Caroline wrapped her arms tighter around Mark and hoped he wasn't able to see or hear anything. Only Ed Turner's hand bled, his gun lying on the floor beneath him. Thad had shot only his hand, which had caused Turner to drop his gun. Despite all the reasons he had to hate and want revenge for his parents' murders and his son's kidnapping, he hadn't killed the man.

She stared up at him, stunned by his action and his compassion. He had stepped between the killer and the lawmen, protecting him with his own body.

"It's over," he told them all, staring first at her, then the SRT members and lastly at his brother. Ash gripped his gun tightly, its barrel trained on Ed Turner's head. "It's over, Ash."

His breath shuddering out in a ragged sigh, the detective lowered his weapon. He forced his gaze from his parents' killer to his nephew and Caroline. "Are you both all right?"

She nodded, her throat too choked with fear and tears to reply.

"I'll bring in the paramedics to check you out," Ash said.

"No, we're fine," she finally managed to assure him.

"Ed needs medical treatment," Thad said. He had turned back to the man, checking his injury himself. No doubt he had experienced treating gunshot wounds in some of the areas he'd been.

But how many had he treated that he'd actually inflicted?

"Why didn't you kill me?" Turner asked. "Because it was what I wanted?"

Thad turned to her and Mark then. And she knew it was because of them. He hadn't wanted to kill a man in front of his son, not even to protect his son.

She couldn't believe she had once had doubts about his ability to be a parent. He was a better one than she could ever hope to be. She needed to tell him that and so much more.

But he turned away from her again and told his brother, "Get her and Mark out of here. Take them to the estate."

She glanced around at the broken windows and doors and the Christmas tree she would never be able to salvage by morning.

Cuffs were already being slapped on Turner's wrists despite his injury. He wouldn't get free again; he was no longer a threat.

As if Ed Turner had seen her lingering fear, the older, broken man spoke to her. "I'm sorry."

She couldn't absolve him of his sins. She could only gather up her son in her arms and follow his uncle out to a waiting patrol car. She glanced back at Thad, hoping it wasn't the last time she'd see him.

Now that his parents' killer would finally be brought to justice, would he head back to one of those countries where he thought they needed him?

Ash caught her backward glance. "I won't let him leave."

"You can't keep him here unless he wants to stay," she said. And that was why she hadn't told him about her love the last time they were together. It was also why she'd fought so hard against falling for him again.

"WHY ARE YOU HERE?" Turner asked as he met Thad's gaze through the holding cell bars.

Thad wasn't really certain himself, except that something had drawn him back to his parents' killer. Despite everything they had said to each other at Caroline's house, it felt as if they'd left too much unsaid, too.

Maybe it was the reporter in him that had Thad wanting answers to more questions. Maybe he'd lived the cover too long. What had made Ed Turner the monster—Marie Kendall's rejection or what he'd done in order to build his wealth and power enough to impress her?

"You're on suicide watch," he remarked.

Ed shrugged. "We both know I'm not going to kill myself. Or I would have done it long ago. I should have done it long ago."

"We all have our reasons for doing what we do," he said with a weary sigh. "What are your reasons, do you think?"

"I didn't kill myself because of Emily," he said. "I never deserved her love or her loyalty.

I never returned it. But I couldn't do that…." He sucked in a shaky breath.

"Why did you kill my parents?"

"I explained all that to you already," Ed said, confusion on his face.

Thad nodded. "You did tell me why. I guess what I really want to know is *how*."

Ed shuddered. "No one needs to know the details of how their parents were murdered."

Thad actually already knew them. He'd read the police files long ago. "I mean *how* did you do it? How did you become the kind of man who could kill?"

"I think you know," Ed said. "And that's why you're here. You're worried that because we might have done some of the same things in the same places that you're like me."

The guy was so smart. How had his life fallen so far apart? Because he'd lost the love he'd thought he wanted without ever appreciating the love he'd already had?

"We did things we had to do over there," Ed reminded him. "To save our own lives and others' lives."

Thad sighed. "We all find ways to justify our actions."

"What's your justification for being here

instead of with your family?" Ed asked wistfully.

Thad suspected that the man wished he could live his whole life over again.

"Fear," Thad admitted. "Fear that I've already screwed up my chance at happiness." Fear that he didn't deserve that happiness at all.

Ed's lips curved into a faint smile. "So what am I, your confidant now?"

"My mission." He wanted more from Ed Turner than just answers.

"I've been that for too long," Ed said. "You let me affect your life for too much of your life."

"Yes," Thad agreed. "So you're going to do the right thing."

"I don't intend to profess my innocence. I want to do the time," he said, "for all my crimes." He shuddered and rubbed a shaking hand over his face. "I can't believe I hurt so many people."

So had Thad, without even realizing he had. Like Ed Turner, he had justified his actions as being for the greater good. How much was he really like Ed Turner?

"It's time for me to face the truth," Ed said,

"without alcohol, without blaming anyone else for what I've done."

Thad breathed a sigh of relief that his family would be spared a long, drawn-out trial.

"Thank you for helping me do that," Turner said. "And don't worry—" he waited until Thad met his gaze "—you're nothing like me."

That was the question, the *fear,* that had brought Thad to the jail instead of home to his family.

"I thought you were," Turner said. "The way you killed Wade. And in all those news interviews, I saw no real guilt on your face. You had totally justified what you'd done. But you were right—it was justified."

Or had he done what Ed Turner had been doing the past twenty years.

"But if you were really a killer, if you really had that darkness inside you that I have, you would have killed me today."

Thad chuckled. "It was what you wanted."

"But you said that wasn't why you didn't kill me."

"I had time to take the shot and the lighting to see your hand," Thad explained. "It wasn't like the night that I shot Wade. It was dark that night and there was so much smoke. And I knew I'd only get one shot." So he'd taken the kill shot.

"You may have had the light and the time today, but you had every reason to want to kill me," Ed said. "I'm the man who killed your parents, the one who terrorized your son and the woman you love. You wouldn't even have to have the darkness inside you to justify killing me. No one would have questioned your reasoning for taking me out with a kill shot." He laughed. "Hell, they would have applauded you, probably even given you a medal."

"If I'd killed you," Thad said, "it wouldn't have been for a medal. It would have been for vengeance." And Caroline would have known it and never forgiven him for killing a man in front of their son. Thad wanted to be a better man for her, a good father to Mark.

"See, you're not like me at all," Ed said. "I gave you something."

"Turner Connections?" he asked with a laugh.

Ed sighed. "No, I've already turned that over to Natalie."

"She'll refuse it."

"Then you can have it. Fold it into Kendall Communications like your brother's been trying to do."

"Don't expect Natalie to come see you," he warned him.

"I've put her on the list of people I refuse to see," Ed said. "I took too much away from her. Affected too much of her past. I just want her to focus on her future."

Thad nodded in agreement.

"You need to do the same," Ed said. "Now get out of here. Go be with your family."

After being gone for so many years, physically and emotionally, Thad wasn't sure he even knew how to do that.

As if Turner could read his mind, he said, "It's Christmas. It's the time for miracles."

Thad glanced at his watch. It wasn't Christmas yet. He had a few more hours until midnight, a few more hours to figure out how to make his miracle happen.

He was gone.

Panic pressed on her chest, stealing away Caroline's breath. She had thought they would be safe here, with Turner behind bars. But the bed where she'd tucked Mark in less than an hour ago was now empty. In fact, the blankets were so smooth it looked as if he'd never slept at all.

Resisting the urge to give in to her panic and utter a scream, she pressed her hand over her mouth and hurried from the room. If she checked every room, she would wake up the others. Pretty much every Kendall had met her and Mark when Ash had brought them to the estate.

Except Thad.

She didn't even know if he'd come home yet. Or if he even intended to.

She could wake up any of the others, though, and they would help her search for her son. But she wanted to check one place first, just in case she was overreacting.

She rushed down the stairwell and through the two-story foyer. She stopped, her mind frazzled as she tried to remember again what was where. The house was so big. Hell, it wasn't a house at all. Nothing with double stairwells and two separate wings of bedrooms could be considered a mere house. The ceilings were so high that noises echoed.

Christmas music, something she never expected to hear in the Kendall household, drifted down the hall. And a deep voice was pitched low, rumbling in a one-sided conversation.

She followed the noises to the family room. The Christmas tree rose to the pitch of the cathedral ceiling. Its twinkling lights reflected back from the wall of glass behind it and cast a beautiful glow across the man and the boy who sat on the couch near the tree. She had thought she might find her son here, drawn back to the tree with which he'd been so awed earlier. She'd never expected to find Thad beneath the tree, too. Mark was cuddled up on his lap, their heads bowed close together over the book father read to son.

Caroline's heart warmed and swelled in her chest. She had to clasp her arms around herself so that she wouldn't throw her arms around them both and never let go. Mark wasn't the only one who'd wanted this for Christmas: family.

He had just been the only one hopeful enough to believe Santa could bring him what he wanted. Caroline had stopped believing in Santa long ago. But not as long ago as Thad.

He finished the story with a flourish of affected voices and special effects. Mark giggled in delight. And Caroline clapped.

"Mommy!" Mark exclaimed. "Daddy was just reading me a story."

"I found him down here by the tree," Thad explained.

"It's so pretty," Mark said with a happy sigh as he snuggled into the corner of the couch where he'd piled pillows and blankets. "Can I sleep down here under it?"

Panic fluttered in her chest again.

"He's safe," Thad assured her. "The whole family's here tonight."

She was surprised that any of them would want to be here tonight of all nights: the twentieth anniversary of their parents' murders. But they had been there when she and Mark arrived, and then they'd decided to spend Christmas Eve together.

But for Thad.

"They keep coming down to check on him," he said, gesturing toward the plate of cookies and milk that had been left on the coffee table for Mark instead of Santa.

"They're going to spoil him," she said.

"Is that going to be a problem?" he asked, studying her face with genuine concern that she might not be comfortable with his family embracing Mark so fully.

She glanced at her son, who was already

drifting off to sleep as he stared up at the tree. "No. I think it's wonderful that he got what he wanted for Christmas."

She leaned down to press a kiss to Mark's forehead. Then she tapped a finger on the book Thad had been reading. "'The Night Before Christmas'?"

"Would you rather I read him something else?" he asked, lifting a brow.

"You can read him whatever you want. You saved us tonight," she said. "And you saved Edward Turner, too."

"Too many people have already died," he said with a weary sigh.

She wondered when he'd last slept. She reached for his hand and tugged him to his feet. "It's Christmas now," she said, noticing that it was after midnight.

"Did Santa bring you what you wanted?" he asked.

"Not yet." But she led him down the hall to the stairs and then up to the suite that was his. She'd been shown to this suite earlier but had refused to assume that Thad would want her staying with him. So she and Mark were staying down the hall in a guest suite.

Except now neither of them intended to stay in there. Mark was asleep downstairs.

Thad's family would watch over him. And she intended to sleep here, with Thad. She reached for the buttons on his shirt, sliding them open so that the material parted and fell away from his chest.

"I'm not Mark," he said, his voice rough as his eyes lit with passion. "I don't need your help."

She froze with her hands raised up between them. "I know," she said. Her son had been the last thing on her mind as she'd bared Thad's heavily muscled chest. "You don't need anyone."

He shook his head, and then he wrapped his hands around her waist, pulling her close to him. "I need you...."

She didn't wait for whatever else he had to say, and he looked as if he intended to say more. She'd heard what she needed, that she was needed. Sliding her arms around his neck, she pressed her mouth against his and kissed him in a way that would leave no doubt that she needed him, too.

Thad's lips parted on a groan, and he deepened the kiss, sliding his tongue into her mouth. Her pulse pounded as desire overwhelmed her. She wasn't the only one losing control.

Thad's hands shook as he fumbled with the belt of her robe and pushed the soft fleece from her shoulders. She hadn't dressed for seduction; as a single mother, she never did. But Thad acted as if her simple cotton nightgown was a see-through negligee. His pupils dilated, his eyes darkening with passion.

"You are so beautiful." The words came out in a sexy rasp.

And for the first time in a long time, Caroline felt beautiful. Acting the seductress, she slowly released the buttons and parted the fabric so that it slid off her shoulders and fell atop the robe.

Thad sucked in a sharp breath. "*So* damn beautiful…"

He was the beautiful one with the lamplight gleaming on the hard muscles of his bare chest and arms. She had to open her mouth to breathe as he literally stole her breath away. Then his lips pressed to hers again, kissing her as if he never intended to stop.

She never wanted him to stop. Never wanted him to leave…but tonight was only about tonight. Not tomorrow, even though dawn was beginning to lighten the sky outside his windows. He acted as if he had all night. He took his time taking off the last of their clothes. Took his time touching her... everywhere.

And kissing every inch of her skin. Her knees weak, she dropped onto his bed, and he followed her down. His body covered hers, slick skin sliding over slick skin.

After kissing her lips, his mouth slid down her cheek, into the hollow below her jaw. She shivered at the delicious sensation. But he moved lower, sliding his lips across her collarbone and over the slope of her breasts. She arched, silently begging him for more. He gave her more, his lips closing over the nipple.

She whimpered as the passion intensified and pressure built inside her. Then his fingers were there, sliding into her, and she arched against his hand. But it wasn't enough, even as she came, to release the most intense pressure.

She reached for him, closing her hands around the length of him. He pulsed and shuddered in her grasp. "Caroline..."

"Take me, Thad...." She was already his. She had always been his.

"I—I don't have any protection."

She didn't care. He had given her the most

precious gift the last time he'd left her; she would be blessed if he left her another.

She parted her legs and arched her hips and guided him to her core. As if his control snapped, he thrust inside her, joining their bodies. Caroline clung to him, wrapping her legs tight around his waist and her arms tight around his shoulders.

Muscles strained along his neck and in his shoulders and arms as he braced himself above her. He stared down at her, his eyes full of awe and something more.

Something she dared not trust in case she was only imagining it. So she closed her eyes and clutched him close. She met his every thrust, taking him deeper and deeper into her body and her heart. Every time she'd thought she couldn't love him any more, she learned to love him more.

The pressure wound tighter, the exquisite pain of it nearly tearing her apart before she shattered. Pleasure, even more intense than the pressure, overwhelmed her. She had never known anything as powerful or as profound.

Thad tensed and joined her in ecstasy, her name on his lips as he buried his face in her neck and his body deep in hers. He clutched her close, keeping them joined, as he rolled to his side and carried her with him, tight in his arms. As if he never intended to let her go.

As if he never intended to leave.

"Caroline," he began, as if he was coming back to all those words she'd seen earlier in his gaze as he'd stared at her.

But she was too much a coward to hear them now, when she was more vulnerable and more in love than she had ever been with him, so she closed her eyes. And she pretended to sleep.

When Christmas came, she would learn if Santa had brought her what she wanted…or if he intended to take it—and Thad—away from her again.

Chapter Eighteen

She was gone.

And Thad had only himself to blame for waking up to an empty bed. He should have told her what she deserved to hear, what she had deserved to hear from him four years ago.

That he loved her. That he couldn't leave her and Mark ever again.

He had dressed and rushed downstairs to tell her those words and had found the house full of people, everyone who mattered to him, except for *her*.

"She's coming back," Aunt Angela said as she pressed a mug of coffee into his hand. "She only went to check on her friend's husband."

"You saw her?"

Aunt Angela smiled. "This morning, when she left. You were still sleeping." And from the twinkle in his aunt's eyes, she knew how Caroline had known he was still sleeping.

She'd been in his arms all night, or what had been left of the night when he'd finally fallen asleep.

"You had to know she was coming back," his aunt persisted as she pointed to the little boy who sat on Uncle Craig's lap. "She would never leave him here."

He grinned at his son. "No, she wouldn't."

"She was going to stop off to get his gifts from their house and bring them back here," Ash said as he and Rachel joined Thad and Aunt Angela. "She couldn't bring them yesterday and risk him finding out the truth about Santa."

Rachel patted his hands, which as always, covered her belly. "I'd say Santa is very real this year."

"Santa Claus brought you something, Daddy!" Mark exclaimed, wriggling out of Craig's lap to run over to where *Santa* stood by the tree.

At the sight of former navy SEAL Grayson Scott in a Santa suit complete with padded belly and snowy-white beard, Thad choked on his sip of coffee laughing. Gray was a great addition to the Kendall family, so loving and protective of Natalie that he would do anything for her. *Anything*.

Just as Thad would do for Caroline, if the stubborn woman would give him the chance to prove it to her. He glanced toward the door to see if she'd returned. But Mark grabbed his hand and pressed the package into it.

"Maybe you should wait for Caroline," Aunt Angela suggested, "if she got you that present."

Thad shook his head. "It's definitely not her handwriting. She writes like an elementary school teacher." Not like an impatient man, which was what the scrawl of his name reminded Thad.

"That handwriting doesn't belong to either of your brothers," Aunt Angela remarked. "Gray—I mean, Santa?"

He shook his head. "Not mine. If you don't recognize it, Thad, maybe you shouldn't open it."

Thad wasn't surprised where the navy SEAL's thoughts had gone. His forayed there, too, wondering yet if his true identity had been revealed after he'd walked off that last mission to come home. But when he inspected the gold-foil-wrapped package, he realized it was a book.

"*The Great Gatsby*. It looks old."

He glanced inside. "First edition."

Ed Turner hadn't just ransacked his suite the day he'd broken into the estate. He'd left him a gift under the tree, one he'd probably thought he would have no further use for if he'd managed to manipulate Thad into killing him.

"Who's it from?" Ash asked as he studied his face.

Thad shook his head, unwilling to ruin the first happy Christmas morning the Kendalls had had in twenty years. The gift didn't bother him, but it might bother the others. "Just an old acquaintance."

Bored with the book, Mark went back to the couch and the game Uncle Craig had been playing with him. He crawled into his lap as naturally as if he'd known the man his entire life.

Aunt Angela squeezed Thad's hand. "He's such a sweet boy and exactly what we've needed around here again. Children."

"We know what we're having," Ash said, raising his voice to draw everyone's attention.

Aunt Angela's eyes lit with excitement. To her, news like this was far more thrilling than opening any present. "Really?"

"We're going to have a baby boy," Rachel announced.

Mark clapped. "Good! Boys rule. Girls drool."

"You're lucky your mother isn't here to hear that," Thad warned his son, but he couldn't keep the smile from his face. He slapped his brother's back. "That's great, you two. Congratulations."

Ash nodded, his green eyes bright. He reached out for Aunt Angela, catching her hands in both of his now. "We're going to name him Connor."

For the son she and Uncle Craig had lost way too young.

Tears glimmered in her warm brown eyes, and Uncle Craig hugged Mark tight. "That's wonderful," he said. "A beautiful gift…just like children are."

Thad gazed around the room at his family. He had never seen them as happy on any other Christmas, not even the ones before his parents had been killed. Only he, missing Caroline, and Natalie, were not completely happy.

He joined his sister where she stood by the windows, staring out onto the snow-covered patio. "Hey, Nat…" He wrapped an arm around her shoulders. "What are you doing over here by yourself?"

Santa had been watching her, too, his gaze full of concern. He started across the room, but Aunt Angela caught him, thrusting a tray of cookies at him. He was already family, but their aunt was giving the siblings a moment like so many they'd stolen over the years as Devin and Ash joined them.

"What's going on, little sister?" Devin asked. He must have also noticed how she'd distanced herself from them, as if she was now an outsider.

"I'm sorry," she said, glancing over her shoulder at Mark, who jumped up and down next to Gray, trying to reach a cookie. Her fiancé lifted the boy easily and held him as naturally as if he was already a father himself. "It's my fault all these horrible things happened."

"It damn well isn't!" Devin corrected her.

"I caused it," she said. "It all happened because of me." She turned to Thad. "That's why your son was kidnapped." She shuddered. "What if you hadn't been able to save him and Caroline? How much different would today be?"

"Miserable," he admitted. "But I still wouldn't

blame you for any of it. It would be like my blaming Mark for what happened. You had no control over what our mother did, or what Ed Turner did."

She sucked in a deep breath and nodded. "I know that. I do." She lifted her shoulders as if finally relieving herself of the burden of guilt she'd carried needlessly. "He's not my father, you know."

"We know," Ash assured her. "You are one hundred percent our sister. You always have been and you always will be a Kendall."

Her quick grin flashed. "Well, at least until I become Mrs. Grayson Scott in a few months."

Thad reached into his pocket for the gift he hadn't yet placed under the tree because the person he wanted to give it to wasn't there. But then he turned away from the window and caught sight of her across the room.

She had returned, carrying her own bag of gifts as if she were Santa Claus. But there was nothing masculine about her red sweater, black skirt and tall leather boots, or all the generous curves he'd kissed and caressed just hours ago.

Their gazes met and held, and his temperature rose at just the memory of her touch, of her taste. He started forward to close the distance between them.

But Uncle Craig stood up and clinked a champagne flute with a spoon. Instead of passing out cookies, Aunt Angela was now moving around with a tray of drinks.

The siblings moved back to the middle of the room and gathered around the man who'd been their rock for so many years. Each accepted a glass of champagne, ready to celebrate whatever he deemed worthy of celebration, which, today, was so much.

"I have an announcement to make," he said. He stopped Aunt Angela, taking the tray from her and pressing a drink into her hand. "It's your present, actually."

"My present?" She lifted her fingers to the diamond pendant he'd bought her.

"Not that," he said. "Your real present, if you think you can handle it."

She narrowed her eyes with suspicion. "What are you talking about?"

"Time," he said. "After everything we've been through the past four months, I've realized how little of it we actually have. So I don't want to waste another minute apart from you, my sweet wife."

She blinked back tears at his compliment and the depth of love for her on his face.

He turned toward the rest of them now. "I'm officially announcing my retirement from Kendall Communications."

Devin lifted his glass. "I understand your reasons," he said as he glanced down at his fiancée, whose hand he held in his free one. "But I don't think I can run the company alone."

Uncle Craig laughed. "We both know that's not true. You've done more with that company than I have, and you can take it even further on your own."

Devin shook his head. "Not on my own." He turned to Thad now. "I need help to take it in the direction I want to go. Are you interested in a job, little brother?"

"I need him at SLPD," Ash interrupted, as if their little brother was a toy the two former rivals used to fight over.

Thad suspected he could do more good at Kendall Communications. But before he could answer, he had to ask a question of his own.

Caroline held her breath, waiting for Thad's answer just like the rest of his family did.

Was he going to stay? Would he give up being a spy to become part of his family's company?

To become a family man?

"Mark," he said to his son, "bring your mother over here. She's the only one who hasn't opened a present yet."

Heat rushed to her face, and she shook her head. "This isn't the time," she protested even as Mark, surprisingly strong for his size, tugged her toward the Christmas tree and Thad. "Everyone's waiting for your answer."

"And I'm waiting for yours," he said, and he pulled a small box from his pocket.

Her heart began to pound out its own version of "Jingle Bells." "I don't understand."

He dropped to one knee in front of her and his entire family.

"What did Santa bring Mommy?" Mark asked his aunt, who lifted him up in her arms.

"Diamonds," Natalie replied with a lusty sigh as Thad opened the box to reveal a solitaire on a delicate band of interlaced gold and silver.

"Looks like tinsel," Mark said in delight. "It's pretty."

It was beautiful, but Caroline didn't care about the jewelry. She cared about the man.

He stared up at her, his blue eyes full of hope and promise and love. Now she no longer feared what he wanted to tell her; she kicked herself for not letting him ask the night before. But somehow it was fitting that he propose here, on Christmas morning in front of their son and their family and the twinkling tree.

"I love you, Caroline Emerson," he said. "I have loved you for years. Leaving you was the hardest thing I've ever had to do. And I've done a lot of hard things over the years. I thought of you every day, wondering what you were doing and if I'd forever lost my chance with you."

Choked with emotion, she could only shake her head. There had never been anyone else for her. There never could be anyone in her heart but Thad Kendall.

"I never want to leave you again," he said. "I want to spend the rest of my life making up for the hurt I caused you. I want to spend the rest of my life giving you the love and devotion you deserve…if you'll have me."

Caroline's heart pounded harder at the look on his handsome face. She'd never seen it on him before: uncertainty. He didn't know how much she'd wanted this, how much she'd wanted him.

"Marry me, Caroline," he implored her. "Please, let me be your husband."

She threw her arms around his neck with such force she nearly knocked him backward into the tree. "I love you, Thad."

He kissed her.

But then one of his brothers pointed out, "She didn't say yes yet."

"Do you blame her?" Natalie asked. "He's kind of a flight risk."

"Not anymore," he promised them all. "I'm going to take that job at Kendall Communications. I'm going to be a nine-to-five company man."

Devin snorted. "Good luck getting those hours."

"Are you sure?" Caroline asked. "Don't give up anything for me. I'll marry you if you work at Kendall or at the police department or even if you feel you have to go back—"

He pressed his finger over her lips as he rose up from his knee and hugged her close. "I'll never go back. I've done what I can over there. I can do more good at Kendall and at home with you and Mark."

She smiled. "I would like a little girl."

"Good thing you're retiring," Angela said to her husband as she leaned against his side. "We're going to be very busy babysitting."

"Very busy," he agreed. And the man who had run a multimillion-dollar corporation sounded delighted at the thought of playing with grandkids. He and his wife were more than uncle and aunt or guardians to the Kendall siblings—they were their real parents.

Thad slid the engagement ring onto Caroline's finger. The diamond and metal twinkled nearly as brightly as the tree, or as his eyes as he stared at her. "Thank you for giving me exactly what I wanted for Christmas," he told her. "Your love."

"Santa brought me what I wanted, too," Mark said, wriggling down from his aunt's arms to hurl himself at her and Thad. His father lifted him up so that he snuggled between them. "A family."

Thad kissed his forehead. "Santa did good this year," he said, and he glanced around the room at his loved ones. "We all got what he wanted."

Love and happiness. There were no greater Christmas blessings.

* * * * *